I Still Don't Even Know You

I Still Don't Even Know You

Stories by
Michelle Berry

Lynn -
my 1st Chapters
customer -
Michelle Berry
Sept. 2010

TURNSTONE PRESS

Turnstone Press
Artspace Building
206-100 Arthur Street
Winnipeg, MB
R3B 1H3 Canada
www.TurnstonePress.com

Turnstone Press gratefully acknowledges the assistance of the Canada Council for the Arts, the Manitoba Arts Council, the Government of Canada through the Canada Book Fund, and the Province of Manitoba through the Book Publishing Tax Credit and the Book Publisher Marketing Assistance Program.

Quotations from the Good News Bible in "Be Kind to your Children" are used with permission. Good News Translation: © ABS, 1976

Cover design: Jamis Paulson
Interior design: Sharon Caseburg
Printed and bound in Canada by Friesens for Turnstone Press.

Library and Archives Canada Cataloguing in Publication

Berry, Michelle, 1968–
       I still don't even know you : stories / by Michelle Berry.

ISBN 978-0-88801-368-2

       I. Title.

PS8553.E7723I88 2010   C813'.54   C2010-901417-0

For Stu, Abby and Zoe

and for Charlie Foran,
whose encouragement came at just the right time.

Contents

I Still Don't Even Know You

Five Old Crows

A black crow swoops by, startling them.
"His liver now," Rosalie says. "Now it's his liver." A spaghetti strap has fallen off her shoulder. Brigitte reaches over to pull it up.

"Mine, it's gas. Flatulence. Bloating." Nancy raises her arms up in the sun. "Farting. Plain and simple."

"Oh God, Victor had that for a long time," Brigitte says. "He'd stink up the room. And he'd never admit to it. What was he thinking?"

Sheila nods. She would like to think she rarely says anything unless she has something important to say.

The ice cube in Nancy's glass tinkles. Warmed by the sun, it slips further into her drink. She looks up the small rise of grass to her huge house. It is lit in the glaring sun. She can't even look at the pool, it's too bright.

"Gin and tonic at two in the afternoon," Nancy says happily. "I'm glad we thought of this. I was getting tired of Diet Coke."

"You can't have a club without alcohol," Sheila says, and everyone nods.

The crow caws from among the bushes.

"It's hot today, isn't it?" Rosalie says. "I wonder if the dresses were such a good idea."

"We could always meet inside." Nancy won't give up the dresses. They were her idea. A brilliant idea. A club uniform, in a sense.

Brigitte fingers her napkin with stumpy fingernails. She hasn't had a manicure in months. Victor doesn't like sharp nails. She looks at her nails, sighing, as she plays with the napkins. Nancy had the napkins printed up with the club motto. Brigitte smiles at hers. If only Victor could see it. Maybe that would hurry the process along, maybe that would kill him off. Brigitte thinks of slipping the napkin into her purse when the other girls aren't looking, showing it to Victor at night and explaining the club to see what would happen to him (heart? stroke?), but then she worries about being found out. After all, she did take an oath. Besides, Victor would only laugh. He's always laughing at her. Like she's a toy. Not human.

Nancy's nails are long and sharp, perfectly manicured. "Shall I call for more drinks?" Nancy holds up those nails and snaps her fingers together. Suddenly a maid appears and bends down beside her. "More gin and tonics," Nancy says.

"Where's Maynard today?" Rosalie asks. Rosalie used to work with Maynard at the law firm. Before she quit and he retired. Only Brigitte knows this. No one else has asked. In fact, Rosalie doesn't even know if the other women ever worked, ever held a regular job. Or if they have spent their fifty or so years with one goal in mind: marry rich. Rosalie misses the firm. Although she likes living her life. She likes her new dresses. She likes her large condominium.

Nancy laughs. "Sleeping. Like a baby. He's asleep. He takes his afternoon nap every day at this time. A goddamn baby. All of this," Nancy waves her arms around indicating the pool, the lawn, the gardener clipping the hedge. She hears the whirr of a lawnmower but she can't see it anywhere. "And he sleeps the days away."

Rosalie stares longingly at Nancy's pool. It's all right for Nancy to have suggested the black dresses because she can swim in her pool anytime she wants. But Rosalie's condominium is for seniors and, even though it's comfortable and luxurious, there are pool hours, rules, that must be obeyed. No one can swim in the afternoon. Like Maynard, most of the seniors are napping. And the afternoon, Rosalie has remarked many times, whenever Frank can hear her, whenever he has his hearing aid in, the afternoon is the hottest time of the day. That's the time of day you *want* to go swimming. Not in the early evening or early morning—the two times you *are* allowed in the pool. With your flutterboards and your bathing caps. All the older women with their fat-hiding bathing suits and little skirted wraps. Cruise wear. Rosalie scowls at Nancy's pool. She hasn't worn a bikini in years. Not that she would anymore, but she thinks she still could. Her body is still fine. A little saggy in places, but nothing to be ashamed of.

Brigitte is sweating. She worries about a stain on her dress. A little, elegant Gucci dress today. Strapless. There will be white salt stains in a half circle under each armpit if she isn't careful. And her shoulders will burn and freckle. Brigitte sighs. At least she has stopped worrying about pantyhose. No use wearing them. She slides her naked feet into her heels and hopes for the best. Last week a little foot powder took the smell away instantly. Victor doesn't ask where she's going on Thursdays all dressed up. He just laughs at her and says, "Black? In this heat?" At his age, Brigitte supposes, he thinks she's going to funerals. Victor forgets that Brigitte is almost half his age.

"Our friends are all dying," he says all the time.

"Your friends are dying, Victor. My friends are only fifty." He laughs. It's amazing, Brigitte thinks, how fifty is now young. When you're married to a man who is eighty, fifty seems like nineteen.

Three weeks now and the Little Black Dress Club has almost run its course. Sheila is tired of it. She has no patience for it. They do nothing but sit in lawn chairs at Nancy's house, sweat in their dresses (a new one every week, of course), sip Diet Coke (or, as in today's case, gin and tonic) and stare at the pool. Sheila thinks most clubs last for about a month before they get boring. The last one they formed, the Shopping Club, lasted two months. But three weeks seems awfully short. Most clubs have a focus. They went shopping in the Shopping Club. And they each had to buy at least one item over $500. Once the LBD Club decided on a motto, formulated a routine (wear new dresses at least once a month) and named themselves, the women lost all energy. Sucked out of them. The heat. The pool. The gin and tonics. Now Sheila's third. Sheila wishes she were still in the Shopping Club. At least the stores are air-conditioned.

"We must have a plan," Sheila says.

Brigitte and Rosalie nod. "A plan."

"What kind of plan?" Nancy asks. She's happy to sit here in the sun; her vintage black number isn't as hot as the other girls' dresses. Nancy likes to see her friends sweat. She doesn't sweat. No matter what. It gives her a sense of control to notice Brigitte's stains and Rosalie's wet-browed scowl as she stares at Nancy's pool.

Nancy has never used her pool. She sits by it in her bathing suit most afternoons, but she's never put so much as a toe in. That would be unbecoming. She worries about the effects of chlorine on her blonde highlights. On her skin. Nancy sometimes feels as if her body and her appearance are her business. As in capital-B "Business." She has to keep herself up, keep the "Business" up. She's not getting any younger. Fifty-two now, although she tells everyone she's forty-nine. Three husbands dead and she has more money than she can count (that's why she has an accountant, she thinks, and smiles to herself), but Maynard hasn't yet signed his over. There's something so addictive, so compulsive about waiting them out, these old men, and collecting their money. Something sweet. That's why she thought of the motto. Although it doesn't apply to her. It applies to all the others. They are on their first husbands. Or at least their first older husbands. She thinks they've each had real husbands. Divorces. Kids somewhere in tow. But now, with the rich, they have only just begun. And that's why they meet at Nancy's house. She's in charge of this club. Just as her body is her Business, this LBD Club is the Board of Directors. She's the Chair. The CEO. Nancy laughs suddenly and everyone looks at her.

"There's nothing funny about it," Sheila says.

"Yes, a plan," Rosalie says. "I think Sheila's right. This is, well, hot. It's hot out."

"A plan." Brigitte nods. Her dyed black hair is attracting the sun. She wonders if her scalp is burning.

The maid comes back with more gin and tonics. She gives Nancy her glass first. She passes around a tray of hors d'oeuvres but all the women deny themselves, even though Brigitte's stomach is growling. She holds her motto napkin tightly in her hand and wills herself not to look at the tray of food the maid has left on the table.

On the way back up to the house, the maid takes a feta cheese stuffed phyllo pastry triangle out of her pocket and pops it into her mouth.

"The motto: Always a Pallbearer, Never a Widow," Nancy says. "The Little Black Dress Club." Nancy pauses. "Is that not good enough? There must be more? Is something wrong with my backyard? With my drinks? With my motto?"

"No, no, no, no, no, no." The women become animated, like birds. They bob their heads and wave their hands.

Sheila says, quietly, "But the motto doesn't make sense."

"What do you mean?"

"We've never been pallbearers, and you, Nancy, you've been a widow three times."

Nancy stares at Sheila. She stares at Sheila's lovely Oscar de la Renta dress. She estimates the cost. At least $1,600. She sizes it in her mind. Sheila's new breasts curve out of the dress nicely, the swelling has gone down. Her stomach bulges slightly, her diamond earrings sparkle. Nancy is pleased to see crow's feet around Sheila's eyes. If there is anyone she has to be careful of, it's Sheila. The other girls aren't even in their category.

"If you don't like the motto," Nancy says slowly, "I can always throw away all the napkins."

"What about…" Brigitte says, "what about: Waiting for Death."

"Waiting for Money," Rosalie says.

"Why are we waiting?" Sheila says. "We should do something."

"That's ridiculous," Nancy says.

"Which one?"

"Both."

The women shake their drinks in their hands. The ice has completely melted. Their drinks are watery and warm.

"Why," says Sheila again, "are we just waiting?" She has a devilish look on her face. A smirk. A grin.

"Well, you can't just go and murder your husband, can you?" Brigitte laughs. She imagines putting a pillow over Victor's head. His old head. Turning off his hearing aid first. It would take only seconds to kill Victor. He would put up no fight. The varicose veins in his legs throbbing. *Goodnight, sweet prince*, she'd say. Or something like that. Press hard. Hold down.

"Why not?"

"Murder." Nancy laughs. "That's not what this club is about. I waited through three husbands, and now I'm waiting for the fourth and—"

"Isn't that what crows are called?" Brigitte says. She points at the crow in the tree. "A murder?"

"Yes, Nancy," Rosalie says. "You waited. And waited and waited." Rosalie smiles at Sheila. "She waited. Why do we have to wait?" She giggles.

"Oh, seriously," Nancy says. She stands up and smoothes down her Chanel Vintage cocktail dress. When she stands she is impressive. The other women hold in their breath. Nancy's blonde hair lights up above them in the sun. Her eyes flash green. Her lips brilliant red. Blood red. "You can't be serious."

Sheila is the only one of them with courage. She stands next to Nancy. Nancy's power is slightly diminished by the size of Sheila's cleavage. The dress clings to her, follows all her curves. "You waited. But we don't have to wait."

"Oh my," Brigitte says.

Rosalie imagines Frank at the condominium. She imagines another early dinner on the patio, a swim in the pool. Early bed. Maybe some TV or a book. A kiss on the cheek. Then they retire to their separate bedrooms. She sighs. And then what? How would she do it? A gun? A knife? Rosalie can't stand the sight of blood. The thought of it makes her feel queasy.

"I've waited for six years," Sheila says. "Rupert seems to get stronger every year."

"Frank is on his way out," Rosalie says, quietly. "It's only a matter of time."

"And Victor," Brigitte says. She's actually become quite fond of Victor. Even if he does laugh at her. At least he does laugh, though. Some of the old men she knows never laugh. Afraid their dentures will fall out, she supposes. "Victor's losing his mind. Why, just the other day he called me Betsy. That was his first wife's name." Victor snuggles up to her at night like a child or a pet. On the porch swing, after a small, easily digestible dinner and some Pepto-Bismol. She likes to pat his bald head. Brigitte is hungry. She reaches for the hors d'oeuvres tray, but changes her mind and puts her stumpy-nailed fingers back on her lap.

"He may change the will," Sheila says. "If he's losing his mind."

"No," Nancy says. "I will not actually kill Maynard. That's not how this works. You must wait. The wait is what makes the spoils more exciting. It's the waiting. The planning. The—"

"That's ridiculous," Rosalie says. "If I wait any longer I'll be too old to get married again. It's just a matter of figuring out how to do it."

Sheila smiles. She sits back in her chair. "I make a motion," she whispers, "that we change the rules a little. Change the club a little. Make it more fun."

"A contest," Brigitte says. "I love contests." She claps her hands together. Her silver bracelets jingle and catch the sun. The crow caws again and swoops out of the tree. "On second thought," she says, "I think it's a lot of crows that are a murder. Not just one."

"I simply refuse." Nancy turns her back and looks up at her impressive house. It's not that she wouldn't want Maynard to die right this instant—stop his whining and snivelling about his sore back, his aching prostate, his stiff arthritis, stop the incessant snoring and stomach pains—*I can't eat red pepper anymore, I can't eat spicy food, everything gives me gas*—but the game is in the wait. "What are you proposing, anyway? We poison them?"

The maid appears suddenly and again tries to pass around the tray of hors d'oeuvres. The spinach dip has gone slimy in the heat. The maid's forehead is shiny. Not one of the women takes any of the food. The maid sighs. She pockets another pastry. No one sees her do it.

"We can't all do the same thing," Sheila says. "That would be suspicious."

"Ridiculous." Nancy sits again, smoothing out her Chanel number. She got a good price on it. Her personal shopper called to tell her about it. Only worn once. "You are all simply ridiculous."

"Shopping for a funeral must be fun," Rosalie says, dreamily. "Think of the dresses. The hats. The shoes. Gloves even."

"Gloves," Brigitte sighs. "In this heat? And of course we'll have to wear black. I'm getting tired of wearing black. Can you wear dark blue to a funeral?"

Rosalie stands and walks towards the pool. Her shoulders are burned and now she has spaghetti strap lines. Her dress is one size too small and shows her panty lines. Her large underwear. The kind that suck her stomach in. They don't really work, but she'll try anything these days. The gin and tonics have made her woozy. No food today has made her woozy. She sways in her heels on the clay tiles around the pool. The blue water is mesmerizing. Rosalie leans forward. She wants to dive in.

"How would you do it?" Brigitte asks Sheila. "If you were going to do it?"

Sheila thinks a bit. She swirls the ice cubes around her glass. She pictures Rupert in her mind. His nose hair and ear hair. The only black tufts on his body. The rest of his hair is white. His dandruff. His fumbling old man hands in bed. Trying to do something, anything. Getting nothing done. The sight of her $10,000 breasts is enough to tire him out. He looks and looks but nothing for Rupert works anymore.

"In bed," Sheila says. "A pillow, perhaps?"

"I thought of that," Brigitte says. "I thought of a pillow too."

"Can't they tell, though? Can't the coroner tell if someone has died of suffocation?" Nancy asks. "And you'd have to hold him down. What would you do? Strap him to the bed? You are all being so silly. It's the gin and tonics. You're all drunk."

The maid walks away towards the house. She glances at Rosalie standing close to the pool. The crow swoops down to the side of the pool and looks at its reflection. Rosalie laughs and claps her hands.

"Look at the crow," she shouts.

The maid fights the urge to push the woman in black into the pool. She continues on up to the big house.

"Well," Nancy says. Sheila is staring at her. She feels uncomfortable. Even if this is her house. Her yard. Sheila's glare is discomforting. "If you are all settled then, if that's the route you want to go, we have to get organized. We'll have to figure this out."

"A new motto," Sheila says.

"Napkins?" Brigitte asks. "Or something else?"

"What about jewellery?" Rosalie calls out. "A ring. Like in a sorority?"

"Skull and crossbones," Nancy says. She laughs. Why not, she thinks. At least they can have a contest. She doesn't have to do anything. See which one dies first. The other girls won't have the courage. And Maynard is much older than the other men. She'll win, Nancy thinks. She'll definitely win. "A tattoo?"

Sheila scowls. "Be serious."

"Let's form a committee," Rosalie shouts.

"She's drunk," says Brigitte. "She's going to fall into the pool."

"A committee of two of us to study what we should do. Really look into it. Legal stuff. Likelihood of detection. How we go about it."

"She used to be a lawyer," Brigitte says, nodding toward Rosalie, on the edge of the pool. "Before she married rich. Oops, I wasn't supposed to tell you that."

"Really?" Sheila says. "I didn't know that."

"That's your problem, really," Nancy says. "You've all got nothing to do. So the waiting feels overwhelming. If you'd just wait."

"I have lots to do," Rosalie says, coming back towards the group. Her heels catch in the lawn and little divots of dirt come popping out. "I'm on so many volunteer committees, you'd never even believe. Speaking of which, have you all bought your tickets for the Under the Sea Charity Dance?"

"You have to get out of that seniors' condominium, Rosie. You really have to. It's sucking the life right out of you."

Rosalie looks at her chair. She sits in it. "Frank likes it there," she says. "And they take care of everything for you. The cleaners. Laundry. All the maintenance on the condo. There are cooks who will make every meal for you. If you want." Then she laughs. She indicates her body. "That's why I've turned so flabby lately."

"Ridiculous," Nancy whispers.

"Madame," the maid says, suddenly, startling them. Brigitte jumps and spills her drink. Her black hair is on fire. She thinks she may have sunstroke. Everything around her is blurry. "Mr. Reynolds is awake. He says to remind you of tonight."

"Yes, yes." Nancy waves away the girl. "Tonight, tonight. What about tonight?"

"He says you have cards tonight with the Harriets. At six o'clock."

Nancy groans. "Oh God, the Harriets."

"He says not to wear black, Madame," the maid continues. "He says you look like you're going to a funeral when you wear black all the time. He says to wear red or orange or green or blue or—"

"All right. Enough. Leave." Nancy watches the girl walk across the lawn back to the house. "Silly girl. Never knows when to shut up."

Silly old women, the maid thinks as she walks. Old crows.

The crow dives into the pool and floats around.

Sheila stares at it. "I didn't know crows did that,"

Rosalie jumps out of her seat and walks to the pool.

"Look at it."

The crow swims around like a duck. It caws at Rosalie when she gets close.

"Drowning," Sheila says, suddenly. "We could have a pool party. Drown the men. One at a time."

Nancy fluffs her hair. "Sheila, if all our men die at the same time, it will be suspicious. Don't you think?"

"One at a time." Rosalie leaves the swimming crow and comes back to the group. "That's a good idea. We'll make it a sport. Tell them to tread water and we'll time them. See who wins."

"But you can't have them all die of the same thing."

"What about shooting them?" Sheila asks. "We can go on a hunting trip."

"I couldn't get Maynard to walk to the car, let alone go out into the woods," Nancy says.

"We could hire someone to do it."

"'Bludgeoning,'" Rosalie says. "I like that word. It rolls off the tongue."

"Knives?"

"Pills. That's easy enough."

"Poison."

There is silence. The crow flies out of the water and stands on the grass. It walks up to the women, shaking its wet feathers.

Then, not inches away from Nancy's foot, the crow caws loudly. The women jump.

"I don't know," Brigitte says finally. The heat has defeated her. She's feeling sticky and sad. The gin and tonics have gone to her head and moved down her body. Everything is numb. She thinks of Victor. Of his bald head. She thinks about how he's like a baby, really. An aging baby. He needs her. "I think we should form another club. Entirely. Get rid of the dresses. Something inside. Knitting? Do any of you knit?"

Sheila, Rosalie and Nancy stare at Brigitte. The crow flies off.

The next week the women meet again. This time they are at Rosalie's condo. Not at Nancy's house. Sheila has suggested the new club needs a new location. They sit by the pool. It is afternoon so they cannot swim. They have to whisper as people are sleeping all around them. Again they are wearing black dresses. Each of them in a new one. Looking stunning and severe. And hot.

Nancy won't speak. She's still mad about all of these changes. What fools they are.

"Do we form a committee?" Rosalie asks. "Or not?"

Brigitte's scalp has peeled from the sunburn. She looks like she has dandruff. Her new black dress was only $800 and covers her body. There is white skin dusting her shoulders. She feels as if she's falling apart. Literally, she tells anyone who will listen. "Look at all the skin. Falling. Apart."

Rosalie is also wearing a dress that covers her, especially her shoulders, which are still sore from the spaghetti dress fiasco. It'll take her months to get rid of the burn lines, she thinks. Or longer. She'll have to use the tanning booth in the gym.

"The long and short of it," Sheila says, "is that Nancy is still upset at us. We have to deal with that little problem before we form any committees."

"I spent good money on those napkins," Nancy says. She plays with her new diamond earrings. A small gift she gave to herself to make her feel better about everyone turning against her.

"We can still use them," Rosalie says. Brigitte agrees.

"How? Write on them?"

"That was a silly motto, Nancy: Always a Pallbearer, Never a Widow. It made no sense."

"True."

"That's not nice," Nancy says. "You're not being very nice to me. After all I've done for you. My pool. My house. My drinks. My napkins."

"Of course we all appreciate you, Nancy," Sheila says. "But this time let's have no one in charge. We'll be a small democracy." She laughs. "Not a dictatorship."

"It was my club," Nancy sniffs.

"I've got far too many black dresses now," Brigitte says.

"Can we get on with it?" Rosalie says. She taps her foot on the tiles. She wants to put her foot in the water but she's afraid an alarm may sound. All the rules here in her condominium. The food should arrive shortly, though, and that's good. She ordered from the kitchen last night. She had to bribe the servers to, just once, take off their hairnets when they delivered the food. She gave each of them an envelope. Some cash.

"In our new club," Sheila whispers, "what shall we write about? What do writers write about?" At Rosalie's place Sheila feels as if she's in a hospital. She can't understand how anyone could live here. At least Rupert has that, she thinks; a house, nice cars. He hasn't quite given up yet.

"How do they begin?"

"Do writers form clubs?" Brigitte asks.

Nancy looks at the three women. "A writing club," she says. "Ridiculous."

"Writers wear black," Rosalie says. "And we can keep the same name. I think it's brilliant."

"The napkins?" Nancy scowls. Then she sits up in her chair. Sits up straight. She thinks. "You know. I could write a fantastic novel. I've had so many interesting things happen to me."

"Let's have some ground rules. We'll meet once a week," Sheila says.

Brigitte scratches her scalp. More flakes fall. "Don't writers write alone?"

"And we'll drink Scotch and smoke cigarettes."

Rosalie smiles. "Those herb cigarettes. The kind you get in the health-food store."

"And we'll write things."

"What kinds of things?" Brigitte says. "I think I'll have a British accent."

"We'll write about what we are thinking, what we are doing, what we ate for lunch, that kind of thing. It'll be fantastic." Sheila smiles. "Our new club."

"And then what?" Brigitte says.

"Don't be a party pooper," Sheila says. "We'll decide as we go along."

"But shouldn't we have more of a plan? Will we publish?"

"We may need different kinds of dresses too. Plainer ones. No heels or jewellery. Still black, but we could go to the vintage stores. There's that recycled-clothes store in the mall."

"And committees?" Rosalie asks. "What about committees?"

"I'm not sure if I like the idea of no jewellery," Brigitte says. "What about big, dangling bracelets? At the reading I went to last year in the library the author was wearing big bracelets. They jangled when she held up her hands to make a point. It was striking."

"Yes, bracelets are good," Sheila says. "Does anyone have a pen? I should take notes. And paper. We'll need paper."

"Come to think of it," Brigitte says, "this woman was reading a murder mystery. We could write murder mysteries. Does anyone have any good ideas about that? I think we'll need a plot."

"Oh, I'll be on the committee that goes to readings," Rosalie says.

"A plot?" Nancy says. "What kind of plot?"

"We'll have to read books ourselves too," Sheila says. "A book or two a year. Don't you think? Just until we get the hang of it. Of writing."

"Napkins?" Nancy says.

"No," Sheila says. "We'll just write. And wear black. And drink. And smoke. That will be enough. You'll see."

Mary-Lou's Getting Married

Percy Q is wearing a bright green dress and he's decided to wear it to the wedding even if it will shock the hell out of everyone. He's decided that he looks smashing in bright green, neon green, radiant green, and he's going to walk right out the front door of the house and wear it to the wedding even if Mary-Lou Bishop drops down dead at the altar. He's going to wear it proudly too, Percy Q is, he's going to hold his head high and sashay into the wedding, stroll down the aisle with a look on his face that no one can doubt. Green eyeshadow too and a little dab of green lipstick left over from Halloween. He plasters his face with the guck. Yes, Percy Q thinks as he dabs, this ought to do the trick.

Emmie watches Percy Q from the hallway mirror. She stands in front of the mirror trying to adjust her hat and watches Percy Q's reflection in front of her. He's strolling up and down his room in that outrageous green dress with all that makeup on and Emmie is adjusting her little pillbox hat with the red veil and thinking, "My God." She's thinking, "My God," and her thoughts get stuck there and the pillbox hat falls off for the hundredth time and Emmie shakes her head and watches Percy Q stroll up and down in his room in that godawful green dress.

"We're late," Emmie finally says. "We're late for the wedding and my hat won't stay on."

Percy Q stops pacing and laughs. "Let's go then," he says. "Let's go to Mary-Lou Bishop's horrible wedding."

"Don't laugh at Mary-Lou," Emmie says. She turns to face Percy Q. "You have no right to laugh."

Percy Q checks his reflection a final time in the full-length mirror above his shoe stand and then he waltzes out of the room and heads down the hall, a green nightmare.

"Let's go," he shouts.

Emmie follows closely behind, holding tight to her hat.

"A purse," Percy Q says to himself. "If only I had a matching green purse."

Emmie rolls her eyes and steadies herself on the stairs off the porch. She doesn't notice she isn't wearing shoes and Percy Q doesn't say anything to stop her. Her bare feet pad down the sidewalk as she rushes along, trying to keep up with her younger brother and his violently awful bright green dress with the puffy shoulders and the lacy back. Out on the street, away from the house, they walk quickly, not even looking at each other. They walk to the church and they think their own private thoughts and every so often Percy Q smiles to himself and chuckles, and Emmie's eyebrows knit together and she grits her teeth in anticipation.

Because Emmie knows that, sooner or later, something will happen.

At the wedding Mary-Lou Bishop doesn't drop dead but she does look at Percy Q twice as she trips down the aisle to the altar. Emmie's poor feet are killing her and, after she got over the shock of being barefoot at a wedding, she's wishing she had thought of painting her toenails red to match the veil on her pillbox hat. Emmie's discovered that if she tilts her head just slightly the pillbox stays on and she doesn't have to hold it. So she tilts her head and Percy Q smiles at everyone in his green dress and Mary-Lou Bishop walks down the aisle to the altar, firm and strong. But when she gets to Ted Bubble, Mary-Lou can't help but turn around and look again at Percy Q in his green dress with all that makeup caked on his face.

Percy Q waves. "Yoo-hoo, Mary-Lou," he shouts.

Mary-Lou blanches and turns back to Ted.

Percy Q looks down at his dress and whispers to Emmie, "I wish I had a nice green purse to match this outfit."

"Don't get too used to this," Emmie whispers back. "Don't go crazy on account of Mary-Lou's wedding." She rubs her bare feet together under the church pew.

Percy Q touches up his makeup with Emmie's compact, every so often stopping lipstick application to say, "Amen," "Bless You," and the Lord's Prayer.

Emmie remembers that when he was a little boy Percy Q used to love to stick hay in his shirt and pretend he was pregnant. She remembers that he used to walk up to Mary-Lou Bishop and Sue Master, when they were all just young, and tell them to pat his growing belly, tell them to feel his milk-big tits. Emmie sighs and shakes her head. Now Mary-Lou's tummy is pushing out of that wedding dress and Ted Bubble looks like the proud papa he's going to be and Emmie's brother, Percy Q, is sitting in row five on the bride's side grooming his hair and wearing a green taffeta dress.

At the reception in the basement of the church, Mary-Lou serves the wedding cake to half a dozen people but stops when the baby kicks and cramps up and she suddenly feels nauseous.

"That wedding was not a moment too soon," Mrs. Bishop whispers to Mr. Bishop as they hover over their daughter. They follow the minister down the hallways to a room where Mary-Lou can rest in peace.

In the reception room Ted Bubble stands on the sidelines and watches Percy Q carefully. He doesn't like the outfit that man's got up in. He doesn't like it when people try to be different, try to make a point, stand out in the crowd. Ted Bubble has spent his entire life moulding himself into a plastic replica of his dearly-departed father and he damn well doesn't like it when some fag-boy shows up at his wedding wearing a green dress and godawful green lipstick. Ted Bubble doesn't care if Percy Q is a university man from the big city. He doesn't care if Percy Q just hopped off the train. He drinks his beers and watches Percy Q in his dress and checks on his new bride every so often in the room where she is lying down somewhere in the bowels of the church. Twice Ted Bubble gets lost in the hallways and twice some nice church lady shows him the way back to the beer and the cake.

Emmie has met someone else at the reception who isn't wearing shoes. They laugh about it at first and then Emmie, with her head tilted to keep on her hat, says, "Where are our brains?" and the young man tells Emmie, very seriously, that he was taken captive by aliens and they sucked out his brain, replacing it with red Life Savers. Emmie thinks it's just her luck to be dropped in with the loonies at this wedding. Later, Emmie, with a cramp in her neck, watches the young man's mother drag him over to the bar where she plies him with cola and he spends the rest of the night, wide-eyed and sugared up, dancing barefoot beside the jukebox with Hilly Mount's twelve-year-old daughter, Bets.

Percy Q doesn't know whether to use the women's room or the men's room. He can hear Mary-Lou moaning like a cow down the hall somewhere as he stands in front of the pink and blue doors saying "Eeny-meeny-miny-moe."

Percy Q is a bit disappointed that no one is really taking him seriously in his nice green dress. The red-Life-Saver boy dancing jerkily by the jukebox is sucking up all the attention and Percy Q's makeup is starting to run with the heat. He feels like pulling Mary-Lou Bishop into the washroom and showing her the panties he's wearing under the dress. Emmie didn't want to look at them. Neither did Hilly Mount or Crazy Ethel. It's not that Percy Q wants these women to get a charge out of his undies. He just wants to show them to someone, he just wants to make a point. He feels he's wasted the uncomfortableness of wearing them if he doesn't show them to someone. Percy Q walks into the women's room and enters a stall. He mumbles to himself about undies and dresses and the horrible fact that Mary-Lou Bishop just got married.

Crazy Ethel is talking to Hilly Mount about Percy Q's bright green dress. They are admiring the fabric and the style.

"Take it from me," Crazy Ethel says. "That dress would cost a bundle."

"He always has to outdo us," Hilly Mount says. She looks down at her baby blue dress with yellow buttons. "Go one better. I suppose he bought it in the city."

Crazy Ethel says Percy Q is someone you just can't beat. She reminds Hilly Mount of the haircut he had in high school—the prettiest curls ever, she says.

The wedding goes on into the night. At about 10:30 Mary-Lou Bishop asks to see Percy Q. It's the moment everyone who knows anything has been waiting for. Ted Bubble, who doesn't know anything, looks confused, drunk, out of sorts. Emmie rushes up to Percy Q, takes his hand and says, "Don't be like you are. She's married now."

The jukebox stops playing the chicken song but the young man with no shoes and Life Savers for brains keeps dancing to a tune in his head.

Two days before Mary-Lou Bishop's wedding to Ted Bubble, Percy
Q came home from university on the train. Emmie picked him up
at the station. She was driving the orange convertible through the
snow, top down, and wearing a scarf, looking for all the world like
a movie star. Her chattering teeth were hardly noticeable.

"If you weren't my sister," Percy Q said, as he leaned into the
car to kiss Emmie's cheeks. "I'd marry you." And the mention of
marriage didn't seem to faze him then.

Emmie and Percy Q settled back into the old house as if Percy
Q had never left, as if he hadn't been gone for two years. They
awoke the same time every morning and Percy Q watered the house
plants and made coffee and watched TV and did crossword puzzles
while Emmie worked at the drugstore down the street, behind the
counter, selling cosmetics.

Percy Q wasn't wearing a dress when he got off the train and
he wasn't wearing a dress for the two days prior to the wedding
when he lived with Emmie in their parents' old house in Onion
Corners behind Centre Street just up the block from the Dry N'Sack
Clothes Cleaners where Percy Q had made the money that took
him away to university. In fact, for the first time ever, he looked
perfectly normal. His hair was cut short and he wore no makeup.
Emmie thought that maybe sending him away to university had
finally taken the crazies out of him.

And Emmie snuck her boyfriend, Zeb, into the house both
nights, through the bathroom window, and they made out like teenagers because the whole thing, the sneaking around, was quite the
thrill. Emmie didn't want Percy Q to meet Zeb yet because things
had only just begun between the two of them and Zeb's heart was
a bit weak considering his advanced age. Emmie didn't know what
Percy Q might do yet or what he might be like. She didn't think Zeb
could take the shock of meeting Percy Q because, even though he
was looking normal at the train station, even though she was hoping wildly he'd been cured, Emmie knew at the bottom of her heart
it was only a matter of time before her brother turned.

It happened the second night in front of the TV, a bowl of popcorn on his lap. Percy Q stood up and said, "My God, Mary-Lou Bishop's getting married." He said it as if it had just occurred to him, as if he hadn't come all this way on the train just to attend the wedding.

"And that's not all," Emmie said. She knew it was time to tell him everything. She knew it was time he heard the facts. "She's pregnant, Percy Q."

Things weren't the same after that. No more crossword puzzles or coffee or TV together. Things went all crazy and Emmie sighed a lot and didn't know what to do with her hands.

Emmie is 32.

Percy Q is 29.

And good old Zeb is 75 years old and can kiss like a teenager.

Mary-Lou Bishop shouts, "Percy Q" and Percy Q comes to her in her hidden room in his green dress. He sits beside her on the couch. Mr. and Mrs. Bishop take this moment to go back to the wedding guests.

"We should take her to the hospital," Mrs. Bishop whispers in the hall.

"After," Mr. Bishop says. "We paid through the teeth for this and, goddamn it, I'm going to enjoy it."

"What's going on?" Percy Q asks.

And Mary-Lou cries and says, "The pain's so bad, Percy Q. With all the playing you did at being pregnant when we were kids you'd never have guessed it."

Percy Q looks curiously at Mary-Lou's large breasts and tummy.

Ted Bubble walks in and checks on his new bride, a beer in each hand. He says to Percy Q, "What are you supposed to be?

It's not Halloween, you know." Percy Q smiles nicely and winks. A real wink, a wink that gets into the groom's head. Ted Bubble gets the message. He knows when he's looking at a messed-up man, and leaves the room in a hurry, again getting lost in the halls of the church. But this time Ted Bubble is led into the supply closet by a lusty church lady who tells him he's manly and big and beefy. She wraps her bony arms around his large waist and he puts down his beer and grabs onto her for dear life. It's been awhile since he's been embraced and that Percy Q winking thing really confused him. It made him feel all funny inside and, just for a second, it made him feel good. Ted Bubble does what his dear father would have done in a situation such as this, but he uses a condom he's got stashed in his wallet because, after all, he is married now and has responsibilities. After all, Ted Bubble thinks, he's going to be a papa.

Percy Q lies down on the couch next to Mary-Lou and looks at the ceiling. His green dress billows over her white one and the rustle of the two materials sounds cool, like liquid. Every so often Mary-Lou Bishop-Bubble screams out in pain and Percy Q quits his daydreaming and offers her his hand.

"Remember when we were young?" Mary-Lou pants.

"You had those high heels I wanted," Percy Q says. "And that diamond tiara, whatever happened to that?"

"Oh, Percy Q. You were always so different, weren't you?"

He laughs. "Me? I was the normal one. The rest of you were different."

"How's university, Percy Q?" A pain shoots through Mary-Lou, turning her face purple.

But Percy Q takes her mind away from the ache and tells Mary-Lou about school and his courses and how his dry cleaning money has just about run out. Every so often Mary-Lou groans so loudly she drowns out her husband's joyful cries in the supply closet just down the hall.

Emmie decides the next best thing to no shoes is no hat. She takes her pillbox hat off and puts it on a chair where it gets sat on immediately by Hilly Mount's fat son, Jacob. He squishes it to a pulp but Emmie doesn't care because the hat was uncomfortable and she thinks her head may be permanently tilted and she wonders if Zeb will like her any better for it.

Emmie doesn't know what she's doing with a seventy-five-year-old boyfriend but his kisses send fire into her heart and he owns half the drugstore and might get her a raise. Besides, Emmie thinks, she's stuck in Onion Corners living in her parents' old house, helping her brother make something of himself—why shouldn't she be thinking about her future, her dreams of owning the drugstore someday, living in Zeb's big house on Portland Street? Problem is, in all those dreams of the future, Zeb is long gone and dead and Emmie's got herself a new boyfriend, maybe Jake from the Five N' Dime, and a brand-new pillbox hat that stays on her head. It's not as if Emmie doesn't love Zeb, it's just that she knows he's not long for the world.

Percy Q was a strange child, unable to do anything right from the day he was born. When he was two he talked backwards, mixing words around, saying "There, hey, you, hello," instead of "Hey there you, hello," and walking lopsided and crazy down the street, running when he should have been walking and vice versa. But Emmie and her mother loved Percy Q all they could because there was some little spot of gold right there, deep in his eyes, that shone out and blinded them with its brilliance. They knew Percy Q had something special in his heart and they watched him grow and doted on him, teaching him right from wrong and black from white.

"He's just a little backwards," their mother used to say. "He just doesn't know his way around the block yet."

Percy Q's real attacks of craziness, of sheer weirdness, when they both knew something was wildly wrong, started when he was five years old. Emmie remembers Percy Q sitting in the booster seat at the table wearing only a sock on his little private part and exclaiming that the carrots placed in front of him were *crazy bee-bop baloneys*. They wanted to think it was all fun and games but Emmie's father said Percy Q was *loony*, and when he went to school the teachers said he should be placed somewhere with facilities to take care of children in his situation.

Emmie sighs. She shakes out her head and looks down at her squished pillbox hat and thinks maybe tonight she should let Zeb touch her belly button like he's been wanting to. Emmie thinks she's not that kind of a girl. She thinks she's saved it up for so long she doesn't want to just let it go, but she knows that living in Onion Corners, working in cosmetics on Taylor Street is not something she wants to do for the rest of her life. Belly button touching or no belly button touching she'd eventually have to let Zeb into her bed and take him where he wants to go. And if his kisses are any indication, it might not be all that bad.

Percy Q and Mary-Lou have been together for ages in that back room in the basement of the church and suddenly there is no sound coming from behind the big, oak door. No howling. No moaning. Just stillness. A calm.

It's late in the night and Ted Bubble is sitting on a hard-backed chair in the reception room drinking his tenth beer and thinking it's about time he headed home and put his pajamas on and snuggled into his baby-blue bed under the hockey posters and spaceships hanging from his ceiling. And then Ted Bubble remembers that he's going to have a baby and he's a married man and his heart does a little dance in his chest and he feels slightly ill from all the beer.

The church lady who cornered him in the supply closet wants him again but there's no way in the world Ted Bubble can even get up from his chair let alone find someone to lend him a condom. The world is spinning so much he wants to lie down and sleep.

Ted Bubble remembers that he only slept with Mary-Lou once before she got in the family way, and he is wishing that his little guys, his sperm, had picked a more normal girl to impregnate. Someone nice-looking, maybe. A good cook with large breasts. But Ted knows that his father, rest his soul, would have wanted him to make an honest girl of Mary-Lou and so he's sitting in the basement of the church watching a jerking crazy boy with no shoes dance to the beat of the jukebox. He wonders what's keeping his bride and what she's doing with that university man in the green dress. Ted can't believe they once were in love, Percy Q and Mary-Lou, even though he's seen their initials scratched in every desk in school and around all the town's walls since he was a little boy. He wonders if his new bride changed Percy Q into the fag-boy he is and he hopes like mad that nothing that horrible ever happens to him.

Percy Q + Mary-Lou.
    Mary-Lou + Percy Q.
    P + M and M + P.

Percy Q pledged Mary-Lou his heart and said he'd be back for her, said he would love her forever and would carry her soul with him wherever he went.

"Oh, Percy Q," Mary-Lou says. The pains in her belly have come and gone and she is lying next to him on the couch in the church holding hands and thinking of everything that's been happening to her lately. "You look nice in green."

Percy Q looks down at his dress. "Yes, I'd have to agree." He laughs.

"Emmie's hat looked nice."

Percy Q nods.

"Why did you leave me?" Mary-Lou says. She sits up on the couch and takes his head in her hands. She squeezes tightly.

"Ouch."

"You said you wouldn't be gone long."

"A university education takes a few years, Mary-Lou. Especially for someone as backward as me."

Emmie is dancing with the jukebox, cola-ed up boy with the Life Saver brain. She thinks, after her second glass of wine, that he's quite some catch. She can't believe her luck. Emmie never drinks alcohol but Percy Q's been gone for a while and she doesn't want to walk home alone in the dark. She's stuck in a crummy basement room with a lot of the people in the town she'd rather not talk to. In fact she's heard several of them talking about her and Zeb and it's made her slightly angry, like she could knock over a couple of people. So she has decided to try a little drinking and see what it feels like.

Emmie spent everything she had on Percy Q's first set of encyclopedias. She bought him every stitch of clothing he's worn since their parents died. Percy Q has it made, Emmie thinks. She wishes now she had taken all that money, all the money she's ever spent on him, and moved away from Onion Corners to begin again. Stuck here, Emmie is. Stuck like there are so many leeches on her skin. And the blood's being sucked out of her every minute of every day. Why else would she be dreaming about an old man? Why else would she be in love with his wrinkled face and dry, toothless kisses?

It's not that she doesn't love Percy Q (or Zeb) but, come to think of it, Percy Q's been gone two years, away in the city, and he didn't even send her a postcard. He traipses off that train, looking like a satisfied seal, and he puts on a green dress and does the crazy things that Emmie sent him away to get out of his system.

Emmie thinks maybe Mary-Lou Bishop is the cause of all the suffering in her life. Maybe if Mary-Lou Bishop had never been born, Percy Q would have got on the right track and carried on down the line, moving up, moving ahead, and taking Emmie with him to the big city.

But then she remembers Mary-Lou came along well after Percy Q was walking and talking funny, well after he'd been wearing godawful colours on his face and shaving his eyebrows. Mary-Lou Bishop moved into town the Saturday before Percy Q's eleventh birthday and, although he was never sane to begin with, Percy Q's been crazy and foolish and in love ever since.

That's why Emmie is having a hard time understanding first why Percy Q left town without Mary-Lou tagging behind, and second, why Mary-Lou ended up rolling in the hay with a loser, a drunk, like Ted Bubble. And it's all come to a head tonight, in the church basement, with Percy Q in a green dress and Mary-Lou in white, moaning loudly and carrying on, a baby about to be born.

Good thing, thinks Emmie, that Ted Bubble doesn't know anything. Good thing Ted Bubble is drunk, passed out, asleep in a chair by the jukebox.

But Mary-Lou's labour pains have stopped. She's not having a baby yet, and she is sitting up and craving cake. She's craving anything baked, biscuits or doughnuts or cornbread or muffins.

"We really should talk about all this," Percy Q says. "We really should sit down and have a long chat, have it all out."

"Talk about your dress?"

"No," Percy Q says, although he has been wanting someone to comment on it. "About us."

"You took off, Percy Q. You left me high and dry."

"But I was always coming back. I told you I would come back."

"And how was I supposed to know that?" Mary-Lou gets up and paces the small room. "How was I supposed to know that? You tell me. Two years, Percy Q, two years and nothing from you, not even a letter." Mary-Lou stops pacing, puts her hands on what were once her hips but now are swallowed up by the baby's legs and arms moving around and around in its sac, excited by the noise of the world. "What was I to do?"

"Not Ted Bubble, that's what you shouldn't have done." Percy Q bites his lip. He feels like crying. His makeup would be ruined, he knows, so he just bites his lip and lies on the couch.

Mary-Lou and Percy Q were like this: They were like two peas in a pod, two bugs in a rug, two cats in a cradle. They took one look at each other, Percy Q with his longish, curly hair and backwards walk, Mary-Lou with her imposing nose, her pimply complexion, and they both knew instantly that here was someone else who was pushed out of public life—*here* was someone else. And Mary-Lou's complexion cleared up suddenly and Percy Q walked straight forward and his words came out coherently.

Emmie remembers Mary-Lou and Percy Q sitting on the swing in the backyard. She remembers they made their own little sounds, their own little laughter. She remembers thinking that this is true love, that two people who communicate like this, in barks and squeals, must really be made for each other.

Last night, after Zeb snuck in, Emmie asked him if he loved

her and he put his teeth back in and said, "I'll have to think about that, honey." Emmie told him to climb back out that window and not come back until he could say yes to everything she asked him from then on.

And now she's dancing with the Life Saver boy and his mother is hollering, "Go to it, sonny," and Hilly Mount and her kids are clambering all over the place, screaming because it's two in the morning and the bride hasn't come out to finish cutting the cake, to serve ice cream and lemonade. Ted Bubble is asleep in his chair and little Bets is picking up dirt from the floor and placing it ever so carefully in Ted's wide-open mouth, jumping back when he snores.

The wedding of the century, Emmie thinks. This is a wedding we'll all remember.

Mr. Bishop has had too much to drink and Mrs. Bishop is trying to get him to stop pawing her in public while she's talking to Betty-Ruth and Irene MacDougall from the bowling league. She slaps his hands and says, "Oh my, Donny, not here."

Percy Q and Mary-Lou are back to sitting on the couch and holding hands. They can't believe no one has been in to check on them for a while. They can't believe they are finally together again after two years apart.

Percy Q wants to take off his dress and throw it in the wastebasket. He suddenly feels silly. But he's only wearing women's undies underneath and, even though he likes to shock people, he doesn't think the weather is warm enough tonight for him to go *commando*, wear no underwear. He has shown Mary-Lou the undies and she giggled like she was supposed to but her mind told her to feel sorry for Percy Q because, even though he's a university man, he still is a little crazy at heart and probably won't get anywhere in life.

Mary-Lou thinks about her big, lumbering, new husband, the Ted Bubble she's just married, and she knows that, even though her life will be miserable with him, at least he'll be able to put food on the table. He's got a good job as a carpenter and he's built up a clientele he says would knock her socks off. That's what he told her. Ted Bubble brought over his resumé, typed finely on purple paper, when she told him she was pregnant with his child. He showed her his craft, showed her pictures of the shelves he'd built, tricky ones, corner ones, and he said he had to do the right thing by her and they agreed on it, even though Mary-Lou had an uncommon urge to phone his references first.

Mary-Lou is thinking like this only because she has to.

They met at the dance hall on a Sunday night in June and Ted Bubble had too much to drink and forced Mary-Lou to go all the way. And, even though she didn't really want to, it had been over a year since she'd heard from Percy Q, so she opened her thighs and let the big man in. Here it is, February, and she's pushing out of her wedding dress like she's going to explode.

What's funny to Mary-Lou is that no matter how many times she did it with Percy Q—in the field by the school, in Mr. Richard's barn under the hay, in his own backyard under the porch, she never once got knocked up, she never once felt that squirmy sick feeling she's felt for this entire pregnancy. And Mary-Lou thinks this is funny because she loves Percy Q with all her heart and isn't that, isn't love, supposed to be what babies are all about?

Emmie wants to go home, so she wanders down the corridors of the church feeling sick from wine and getting lost. She comes upon the minister sitting on the toilet in his bathroom, apologizes and moves on, opening every door that isn't locked. Eventually she finds Percy Q and Mary-Lou. She finds them by hearing them talking, whispering and laughing, and she barges in and takes Percy Q's hand and says, "Let's go home."

But Percy Q doesn't want to leave.

"Where's your hat, Emmie?"

Percy Q knows that the second he leaves Mary-Lou she'll have to go home with that big Ted Bubble idiot and she'll be married until the day she dies. He feels consumed by worry. He feels all achy inside.

The problem for Percy Q is that university in the city was so far away from Onion Corners and it made him feel big and good and smart. He went to his classes every day and, even though he didn't understand half of what was being said, he'd lie on the lumpy bed in his rented room at night and imagine himself with a degree. He'd imagine the jobs he would get, the places he would travel. And then, of course, when he failed, bombed all his courses, he couldn't tell anyone about it. How could he face his sister? How could he face Mary-Lou? So Percy Q got himself a half-decent job in a dry cleaners in the city. He was meaning to bring Mary-Lou to his side when he made some money, when he coughed up the courage to tell her about his mistakes, but the embarrassment of the whole thing left him dry in the mouth. Then the job ended, the dry cleaners closed down, and Percy Q wandered the streets, picked through the city garbage, sold what he could find to get by. When he got the telegram from Emmie asking him to come home, telling him Mary-Lou was getting married, he headed home on the first train.

The green dress is from a dumpster behind the Village By the Pond Mall in the big city. He found it last Tuesday with a rip down the side and he patched the rip, and was intending to give it to Mary-Lou for a wedding present. But when he really thought about the fact she was getting married to someone other than himself and then, to make matters worse, found out she was pregnant, Percy Q went a little crazy, dove off the deep end, and put on the dress and the makeup and marched down the aisle back into Mary-Lou's heart and right into her wedding.

When Emmie finds them they are holding hands.

"Oh dear," she says. She steadies herself on a chair. The soles of her feet are black from the dirty church floors. She takes Percy Q's hand and says, "Let's go home," but he doesn't budge from the couch. Instead, he pulls Mary-Lou towards him and hugs her tightly.

"Oh dear," Mary-Lou sighs.

"I have to tell you how it is," Percy Q says to Emmie and Mary-Lou. "I have to tell you both so you'll understand."

Emmie sits down in a chair. She can't wait to hear what's going to come out of his mouth. She's had too much to drink, more than ever before in her life and she's feeling sick and fed up with having to take care of Percy Q. It was one thing when he was a kid, it was another when their parents died, but now he's a grown man, a university man, and Emmie knows that if Ted Bubble sees him holding hands with Mary-Lou he's going to beat the heck out of him and there's nothing Emmie can do to save him. She has to save herself now, she thinks, get Zeb to marry her and then wait until he dies so she can inherit half the drugstore. She might, she thinks, ask that Life Saver boy to come over when that happens. She might ask Jake from the Five N'Dime to drop by the big house on Portland Street. But then thinking of Zeb biting the dust makes her choke up and feel like crying.

Just when Percy Q wants to tell them both about his deception, his lies, how it felt to be out of work in the big city picking through garbage, there's a holy commotion in the hallway and half the reception, what's left of them, barges into the room.

"What's going on?" Crazy Ethel shouts. "Did the baby come?"

Everyone is silent suddenly because, although it was incredibly obvious to them all, no one was supposed to mention that Mary-Lou Bishop was pregnant. It was going to be one of those things where, years later, numbers would be added and subtracted and everything would be made to look right in the world. The townspeople would do it for the baby. It's hard enough, the town agreed, being born without having to go through life attached to an immoral problem.

When the reception people, including the Bishops (the Mr. pawing and clawing at anyone who is near, male or female), enter the room, Percy Q stops what he is about to say and stands up.

"Where did you get that dress?" Tacoma, the church organist, says. "It's such a beautiful colour."

Emmie throws up her arms. At least with her brother's dress no one has noticed her bare feet.

Mary-Lou looks around for Ted Bubble. "Where's the groom?"

No one seems to know where he is until twelve-year-old Bets says he's sound asleep beside the jukebox with a cup of dirt in his open mouth.

Mary-Lou says the baby was just testing her, just seeing if she can take the pain, preparing her for the big day, and then she gets up from the couch, takes Emmie's hand in hers and Percy Q's hand in the other and stands them in front of all the townfolk who are waiting to eat the cake.

"I want to say something," Mary-Lou says. She clears her throat, which is sore from howling and crying out in pain.

"Quiet everyone. Speech. The bride's making a speech." This comes from Jacob, the boy who sat on Emmie's hat, the boy who is a little younger than nine, fatter than an old cow, and can't believe his luck at staying up till all hours of the early morning.

Mary-Lou waits for silence and then begins. "You all know," she says, "that I've been mooning over Percy Q for years and years."

Percy Q blushes. He can't help himself. Somehow Mary-Lou's large bulk makes him feel important and her words send shivers up and down his spine.

Someone shouts, "Hear, hear."

Someone else comments on Percy Q's dress and how it must be all the rage in the big city.

"Well," Mary-Lou continues. "Even though I'm in the family way"—he pats her belly—"even though this baby is Ted Bubble's baby"—she shakes her head mournfully"—even though I just got married a couple of hours ago—"

Someone shouts, "Where's the cake?"

"—I've decided that I don't want to be married anymore and want to stay true and faithful to Percy Q until he's finished his degree."

Percy Q sits down on the couch again. He puts his head in his hands.

Emmie looks around the room and then down at her bare feet. She can't believe her little brother might get married before she does. She's going to have to whip that old Zeb into shape.

Ted Bubble picks that time, just that second, to wake up. He spits the dirt out of his mouth and then grumbles quite loudly. He looks around the empty room. Only the Life Saver boy is still there and he's dancing quietly in the corner.

"Where is everyone?" Ted asks, but the Life Saver boy can't hear him because his mind is full of little candy circles in green, red, yellow and orange.

Ted then searches the halls of the church basement. He gets lost in the boiler room for a minute and then he, too, catches the minister sitting on the toilet, but he finally finds the whole room of people gathered around his fat-bellied wife and that stupid Percy Q in the green dress. Something's going on, he thinks, something he doesn't much like.

Emmie groans when she sees Ted Bubble walk into the room. She groans when she hears what Percy Q says next, his back to the door.

"I love you too, Mary-Lou," he says. "But I'm not a university man." Emmie sees all her hard work, her suffering, going down the drain. Every penny she saved, every penny she gave him, poof, up in smoke.

"What do you mean?" Mary-Lou looks startled.

As Percy Q explains the last two years to the crowd, his

humiliation, his constant devotion to Mary-Lou, Ted Bubble gets angrier and angrier, because all he can think about is the fact that the guy in the green dress just told his new wife that he loves her. Ted Bubble can't remember if he's ever told Mary-Lou that. His head aches from all the beer and his mouth is gritty from dirt. He roars and lunges and the sea of people parts and Ted Bubble attacks Percy Q, ripping the green dress into shreds and bloodying his nose.

There is hoopla, there is chaos, there is wildness. Hilly Mount's kids take to beating each other up and Mary-Lou throws a chair at Crazy Ethel because, out of spite, the woman is pulling Percy Q's lovely puffy shoulders off, ripping at the green material. Emmie stands back, by the couch, careful not to get her delicate toes trampled upon.

Zeb is standing up beside his bookshelf at home, leaning on his cane, scouring his mind for the quotation he used to ask his sixth wife to marry him. He can't remember if it was Shakespeare or Marlowe or Donne. He can't remember and he can't ask her because she died two years ago of old age.

"It's a pity," he says to himself and then he starts to shake because he can't get over his luck having such a pretty girl like Emmie to love him. Such a pretty girl must certainly have a pretty belly button, he thinks, and he quivers so much that he has to sit down.

When the brawl is all over Percy Q lies on the floor groaning and holding his nose. Emmie triumphantly holds up the chair she used to bang Ted Bubble over the head and knock him senseless. Everyone else stops fighting and starts laughing and shaking their heads. They are amazed at Emmie, still protecting her brother after he lied to her about university, and they suddenly forgive her for fooling around with the oldest, richest man in Onion Corners.

"It must be love between them two," Irene MacDougall says to Mrs. Bishop, as they wipe the sweat off their brows. "What else could it be?"

When the minister finally comes out of the bathroom, everything has been cleaned up. Ted Bubble is back in the chair, still knocked out, beside the jukebox in the reception room. It took six men to move him. The music is still going and the kids are all dancing. It's four in the morning.

Mary-Lou asks the minister to annul the wedding. She says she doesn't care if Percy Q is a dry cleaner's boy for the rest of his life, she's loved him fiercely since she was eleven years old. She says he makes her world crazy and happy and fun. Percy Q dances around in his ripped, blood-splattered green dress and hugs and kisses Mary-Lou like there's no tomorrow, he pats her little growing baby belly like it's his. The minister won't annul a wedding until the groom is awake and he wonders aloud how this tragedy will affect the little unborn Bubble. Mary-Lou and Percy Q say they can wait. They say the baby won't know the difference, they say it'll have two papas instead of one. They say they've waited their entire lives to be together as husband and wife, one more night won't matter. The baby in Mary-Lou's belly kicks and jumps and hiccups, as if it's telling the town that everything will be fine and dandy, and Mary-Lou and Percy Q look lovingly into each other's eyes.

A couple of months later Emmie is sitting, barefoot, in Zeb's lap and he's playing with her belly button in his huge house on Portland Street. She's found that she can't wear her shoes anymore. They feel uncomfortable and small, something she never noticed before. Zeb and Emmie are getting married in the summer and she's decided she isn't going to wear shoes under her wedding dress. She's decided that she isn't going to do anything she doesn't like anymore. She's going to be rich and in love and well taken care of.

Emmie tickles Zeb behind his hairy ear and thinks about how she likes being an aunt to little Quince and that makes up for her disappointment with Percy Q over his university career. She likes little Quince so much that she hopes she can have a baby one day herself. Zeb's already had fourteen of them in his long life so she doesn't see why one more would make a difference.

Zeb used Donne's poem about the compass to win Emmie's hand, the poem about how the compass stays fixed at one point no matter how far the other point wanders. He used that poem, he told Emmie, to make her understand that, even though his eye may wander occasionally, stopping ever-so-slightly on some of the heavenly bodies strolling through Onion Corners, it doesn't mean he won't always be·faithful. It just means he's a man, he says, he can't help himself.

It's the same line he used on his last wife, the sixth one. Zeb figures he's getting old. He figures he shouldn't have to make up new romantic sayings for every young lass who snatches his heart. It's about time he relaxed. It's about time he let his mind take a rest or two.

Mary-Lou and Percy Q are at home, in his parents' old house, lying together in bed with little Quince beside them. They have carved M + P + Q on the headboard of the old bed and they are snuggled down in the warmth of the quilt staring at the new little baby girl.

They can't imagine anything happier. They can't imagine anything nicer. And Quince giggles and coos peacefully beside them, thinking about nothing but milk, milk, milk in her peaceful, wonderfully unformed, tiny mind.

Baby Quince is wearing a taffeta green hat on her head, made carefully from the remains of the dress. It keeps her warm and her parents think she looks beautiful.

"You look like a million bucks," Percy Q tells her. "You look like the Queen of England." And he dabs a little green eyeshadow on for effect.

Nobody worries about Ted Bubble because he's found true love in the bony church lady (who's name is Tiny) and, even though he was wearing protection that night, she's knocked up with another one of his babies and they are soon to be wed. It doesn't matter an ounce to the church lady that when she marries Ted she'll be called Tiny Bubble. In fact she likes the name so much that she whispers it to herself every chance she gets.

Be Kind to Your Children

Mr. Roldo thinks x-rays show he has no heart.

Markus eats Bibles, page by page. When he is completely done an entire Bible, he starts on another.

Noodle starts a dance every morning in honour of her dead father, but after breakfast she sits in front of the TV and watches Markus eat.

Meg is the nurse here. She has a bumper sticker on her beat-up convertible that reads, BE KIND TO YOUR CHILDREN. THEY ARE THE ONES WHO WILL CHOOSE YOUR NURSING HOME. She often wonders why some of the words are capitalized and others aren't. She thinks, who chooses that? Who makes all the decisions? Meg doesn't like to make decisions and so she can't fathom, even for a moment, who makes the complicated ones.

When Noodle first moved in she had spaghetti in her hair. Mr. Roldo picked it out and ate it. His motions were soft and soothing, calming. But Noodle became so agitated that Meg had to lock her in her bedroom and put on the lullaby tape in the office. She had to project the sound down the hall and so she pulled the tape recorder out of the office, the cord taut, and tilted it towards Noodle's room so the *hush little baby* noise would settle down the screaming. Meg used to do that for her mother. She used to hum sweetness into her mother's ears when the world was so close it hurt her mother to think of it.

"You're all in a noodle," Mr. Roldo said.

"Holy, holy, holy," Markus said. "The Lord Almighty is holy!"

And Meg shuffled on her swollen feet, back and forth from the office to Noodle's room to calm her, back and forth.

Every morning Markus starts with a new page. After he's swallowed it, he visits the washroom. Then he goes to the TV room, settles in, and tries another page. Drinks water to get it down.

Even though she's in charge, Meg always wonders why. She doesn't know what to do half the time and there are moments, lying in bed in the dark, her nightgown twisted around her stout form, that she thinks she might be the crazy one. Meg can imagine Markus would make a better nurse than she. He has eaten so many Bibles in his fifty-two years that the words of good seem stuck to his ribs. It's as if he's become a part of the morals.

"'When the Lord your God gives you victory in battle and you take prisoners, you may see among them a beautiful woman that you like and want to marry,'" Markus quotes from the Bible.

Even though Mr. Roldo has no heart, he takes a moment to be still and contemplate.

The *Good News Bible* Markus is working on is 370 pages in length, not including the map index, the subject index and all the other forwarding pages.

"Do you ever start from the back and eat forward?" Meg asks.

Markus's mouth is full.

Noodle says Markus hasn't ever read the Bible. She says that he wants to get into heaven just by ingesting it. And then she wonders aloud what ingesting means and whether you can out-gest.

Today they are going on a field trip. Meg locks up the home. She wants to tie them all together with rope, to make them stay safe, like little children, but instead she has them hold hands. Meg holds hands with Markus, and Mr. Roldo and Noodle take hands and walk up front. Over the parking lot towards Meg's car they walk, the other patients in the other scattered homes throughout the compound around the asylum looking out the windows.

"We're going on a field trip," Noodle shouts. "We're escaping."

Meg requested this field trip several weeks ago when she saw the weather turning golden and clear. She asked Dr. Mayburn if she could take them out, just her three charges, into the sunshine, away from the home. Dr. Mayburn wondered about the request for awhile, the long fingers of one hand holding his chin as if his mouth might fall open. He smelled of wine and garlic, with a cheesy smell lingering behind him somewhere. There were gnats above his head. Meg thought to herself, there's a peach pit rotting somewhere in this room. I just know it.

And now they are in Meg's car. Markus is belted into the back seat next to Mr. Roldo and Noodle sits shotgun next to Meg. Meg starts the car.

"'Once I was looking out the window of my house'," Markus quotes, "'and I saw many inexperienced young men, but noticed one foolish fellow in particular.'"

"Oh?" Meg says, grinding gears. "Which house was that? Your childhood home?"

"He lived all over the world," Noodle shouts. "He told me before."

Meg pops the clutch and the convertible shoots forward and back. Meg's foot has always been heavy.

"Let's take the roof down," Mr. Roldo says. "Not that I would care at all, but it's a beautiful day."

Meg pulls over by the exit to the BETTER LIVING MENTAL ASYLUM sign. PLACE YOUR LOVED ONES WHERE THEY ARE CARED FOR IN STYLE, the sign shouts. And underneath, in smaller letters, AFFORDABLE YEARLY

RATES, GOOD DOCTORS, LIVE-IN NURSES, PATIENT TO NURSE RATIO AVERAGES 4 TO 1.

Meg sighs. Four to one until someone dies, she thinks. Then it's only three to one. Better deal for your money. She gets out of the car and starts to struggle with the roof.

Noodle begins to push the buttons on the radio. Billie Holiday sings the end of "Fine and Mellow," and then, "I Got it Bad (and That Ain't Good)."

"Billie has heart," Mr. Roldo says.

Meg remembers when she was little. When her mother used to take her to dances at the Recreation Centre down the street from her house. All the little babies screaming in the corner while the mothers danced until dawn. Although she herself was young, Meg was put in charge of the babies. Even then she didn't know what to do. She's never known what to do, it seems. Meg would change one diaper and the next until suddenly she was changing only clean diapers, her fingers flying over open safety pins, and the babies kept screaming and spitting up and wanting their mamas, and Billie Holiday was singing heartbreak and sorrow all night long.

Meg gets back in the car.

"Where are we going again?" Markus asks. "I want to make sure I brought enough to eat."

"You've got an entire Bible, Markus," Noodle says. "That takes you a month, doesn't it?"

"We're only going out for the day." Meg turns left out of the exit and heads south to the beach.

"Good God it's fine to be alive," Markus says. He chews on the bits of paper stuck between his teeth.

But Meg has been wondering lately if it is fine to be alive. She's been shuffling with swollen ankles, edema from too much salt, and improper shoes, back and forth down those hospital halls for over twenty years now. She's lived in that room next to the kitchen, one tiny room, for fifteen years, moved in to take care of her mother, just after the debt collector took the house and furniture, took everything but the tiny yellow dresser in Meg's room. Her mother died last year. In the asylum. Died with her head in Meg's lap. And Meg's been with Markus for eight years. With Mr. Roldo for six years, and with Noodle from the moment her daddy died in her arms, one year and three months ago. Noodle, the tiny little woman with the big head and hollow eyes. Her dance every morning is eerily perfect. It is noiseless with large movements and pained facial expressions. She dances to the music in her head.

But Meg wonders if dancing sadly is enough. She wonders if helping others is enough. When, she asks herself sometimes, when will someone help me?

Meg pulls over in the parking lot at the beach.

"This," Mr. Roldo asks, "is it? This is where we are going?" He spits.

"We're going to walk the beach," Meg says. "We're going to get some exercise."

Mr. Roldo holds his chest as he gets out of the car and starts to walk down towards the water. x-ray after x-ray but nothing will convince him that he has a heart. "Hear the beating, Mr. Roldo," the doctor says during yearly checkups. "Hear that bumpity-bump? That's your heart, man."

"That's indigestion. That's a piece of fruit travelling through the stomach. That's bile turning in my chest."

"There's no bile in your chest, Mr. Roldo. Just a healthy heart."

Of course if Meg were to think about it, she would liken the old man's failure to admit he has a heart to the fact that his wife is dead. No need to miss her if you don't have a heart. No need to miss. But Meg has no family anymore and she has a heart. Common sense. Meg thinks, she's practical and Mr. Roldo is a romantic. "Surely, Mr. Roldo," Meg says often, "surely you have a heart?"

"'I am wisdom, I am better than jewels; nothing you want can compare with me,'" Markus quotes as he follows Mr. Roldo to the water.

There are several children sitting by the water with their

mothers. Each child has a pile of rocks in their lap and they are throwing the rocks into the water and applauding every splash. "I can do it," one child shouts. "I did it."

Meg stands up at the car and watches Mr. Roldo as he clutches his heart and limps towards the water. She watches Markus, Bible in hand, looking down at his feet. She watches Noodle tiptoe daintily after the two men, watching them closely, never letting her eyes leave their forms. Noodle's dead father seems everywhere around her, watching her. Meg sometimes can see his soul hovering, taking care of his child. Meg wants to get back in her convertible and drive off into the sun. She wants to drive quickly and noiselessly away, her hair blowing in the breeze. It's almost full summer now and she wants to get away fast.

The way these people wallow in their sadness makes Meg tired. Sick and tired. Meg is a trained nurse. She knows they can't help what they do, but lately she just wants to shake them a little, knock them around, tell them to stop it. Stop feeling sorry for yourself, she wants to shout. Stop it now. Meg doesn't know if maybe she wants to say that to herself. Maybe she wants Dr. Mayburn, with his peach-pit gnats, his garlic breath, the cheese smell surrounding him, to raise his hand and slap her. Wake her up. Or kiss her. Maybe she just needs to be kissed. Since her mama died, Meg hasn't been kissed by anyone.

But Markus turns to her, halfway to the water, and smiles. His teeth are black from the dye. His pallor is grey. And it isn't in what he says to Meg but more of the way he looks at her that makes her move away from her car and head down to be with him. To be with them.

"'Give praise to the Lord,'" Markus quotes loudly, "'he has heard my cry for help.'"

"Be quiet," Noodle says. "You're ruining the mood."

"Oh, my empty heart," Mr. Roldo whispers but no one hears him as the children sitting by the water are suddenly noisy and silly. They begin throwing rocks at each other and their mothers shout and holler.

"Let's walk further," Meg says. "Let's walk a little. Let's get away from it all."

The four move on down the beach. They are all wearing variations of white clothing—shirts, shoes, pants, skirts. The asylum outfits are greyish and pinkish depending on what they've been washed with. Meg's uniform is starched so white it shines in the bright light.

"Lookit," one of the children says to his friend as he points at the receding adults. "A bunch of lousy angels."

His friend throws a rock but Meg and Markus and Mr. Roldo and Noodle are too far gone for it to hit them.

Meg's shoulders are high, her walk awkward. She doesn't know quite where she fits in anymore. It seems as if she's more in the middle of this group than on the outskirts and maybe, in this sunshine, walking with this bunch of lousy angels, that suits her just fine. Why should she be in charge? Who, she asks herself again, makes all the decisions in life?

Meg takes hold of Mr. Roldo and tells him, quite plainly, "You know, when I lost my mother last year I thought for awhile that I didn't have a heart. I couldn't hear it beating anymore. I thought it broke. But listen. Put your hand there. Listen with your fingers."

Mr. Roldo places his hand on Meg's bulky chest. He smiles with delight.

"When was the last time," he says, "I got to touch a lady's breast?"

"Hear the thump, thump, thump?"

"No."

"It's there. You hear through your fingers."

"That's silly," Noodle says, starting up with her nervous jittery dance. "Mr. Roldo doesn't have a heart."

Markus opens the Bible to the first page he hasn't consumed and starts to rip off small sections and place them on his tongue. "'You have changed my sadness into a joyful dance,'" he says, his mouth full.

"But it's there," Meg says. "It's the beating of my heart. My mama left it there within me."

"I hear nothing," Mr. Roldo says.

"How else," Meg says, "could I take care of you? You are my children. How could I love you without a heart?"

The group stops and turns to Meg. Stares her down. Markus chews slowly, like a cow, manipulating his mouth around the paper.

Meg laughs.

"'In the beginning,'" quotes Markus.

But then he forgets exactly what he was going to say and Meg says, "Let's move on. Let's just keep going."

I Still Don't Even Know You

They are on the chairlift early that day and Rebecca says her ankle still hurts from the fall the day previously and Jack looks off into the horizon, balances his poles carefully, and taps the front of his skis. A tune. He taps out a tune that makes Rebecca sit up and listen and stop complaining about her ankle. The throbbing, though; that's what Rebecca thinks—and then says: "It won't stop throbbing. Like there's a miniature heart in my boot."

At the top of the lift Jack wants to turn opposite from Rebecca, ski off onto another hill, another chairlift, but this is their first vacation in ten years, their ten-year wedding anniversary vacation, and she wants to talk. And talk she does. That's why, Jack thinks, he wants to be on another hill. What about the tune in his ski, the tapping tune? Or the bird calls? Or the calls of all the kids?— that will come later, they are not up and skiing yet, too early—but soon, the calls of all the kids as they fall down the mountain. It amazes Jack that they do that. Fall. All the time. Up and down, up and down. Especially the snowboarders. Jack would like to snowboard, but Rebecca won't let him. She says he'll break his ankle and then, Jack thinks now, it'll throb. Throb, throb, throb.

The hills are getting shorter, it seems. Two days into the vacation and they've done all the hills and now they know the hills and the hills feel short. The chairlift feels endless. Slowly winding its way up the mountain, screeching and making groaning noises that fill Jack's head. But not enough to overpower Rebecca's chatter. She reminds him of a bird, he thinks. He's never thought that before. Ten years of marriage and suddenly his wife is a bird, a duck— something twittering and honking and… no, not a duck. More like a warbler, a little bird. Because she's small and lean and, well, her nose is a bit beaky.

Not fair, Jack thinks. This is not fair. He's not used to being with someone so much. He needs his alone time. That's what Rebecca calls it. Alone time. Up time. Down time. Alone time. Ridiculous.

And down the hill and back on the lift. Again. Here they are again, seconds later it seems, and Rebecca is talking again. Her sentences stop at the top of the hill, halfway through, and then continue on when they get on the lift. Right in the middle of a word even, she'll keep that train of thought and go with it on the next lift up.

"It's just a little throb, really," she says. She turns her head and looks out from her ski goggles at Jack. He's a bit yellow because her ski goggles are tinted, but he's still handsome. She slides over towards him. Thinks about last night, about the fireplace in their bedroom and how Jack tried to light a fire and couldn't, and how she finally took over, trying not to make him mad, and lit it. She had, after all, been a camp counsellor as a teenager. She spent every summer, all summer, making fires in the wind with little or no firewood for groups of shouting kids. But Jack got all huffy about it and soon Rebecca was wishing she could douse the fire and go to bed.

Lovemaking last night, Rebecca thinks, wasn't up to par. Distracted by the fire, Jack seemed distant. And Rebecca has been worried about her stomach lately, it's getting more pudgy than it used to be. The forty-year-old bulge. She kept trying to hold it in, her stomach, as Jack worked away above her. Grunting. And then she grunted. She knows she did. One big grunt. Because holding her stomach in while moving back and forth, well, it's hard. But probably good for the muscles. Jack looked at her when she grunted. She could feel him looking, even with her eyes closed, and she wondered what he was thinking.

Rebecca takes Jack's hand in hers. His mitt. She can't feel his fingers through all the padding. There are probably only fifteen or twenty people on the lift. They have the lift to themselves. Rebecca talks about what they will have for lunch. Poutine and Diet Cokes. And then where they should go for dinner. The hotel? Into town? Then she brings up the kids. She likes to talk about the kids. All the time. Jack stares off over the horizon. Perfect, Rebecca thinks, perfect to sit up high like this and talk about their two kids. At home with the grandparents.

Up at the top of the hill Jack skis ahead quickly. Rebecca has to skate to keep up with him. Her ankle aches.

"Wait up. Where are we going?"

Jack moves through a path in the trees. Effortlessly. Rebecca thinks he's an effortless skier.

Jack thinks he almost wiped out there. A few too many moguls too close together and the trees are thick. The track through the woods is ungroomed.

They stop together at the top of a hill. One of the harder ones. And Rebecca sighs loudly and says, "It's beautiful today."

Jack looks down, towards the lodge, towards their hotel and thinks he knows he should be feeling lucky. Not everyone can go skiing, he thinks. It's expensive. It's a rich man's sport. But then he thinks, he deserves it. This sport. Because he works hard. Not that everyone doesn't work hard, that's not what Jack is thinking, but that doesn't mean he should deny himself some fun.

Although, lately, skiing hasn't been so much fun. When he skis with the kids they whine about the weather, about their socks, about the fit of their boots. They both want to snowboard, but Jack won't let them. Not until they are old enough to drive themselves to the hospital with a broken neck, he says. Although he knows that makes no sense. Especially since he wants to try snowboarding.

There she goes. Rebecca swoops down the mountain. Good form, Jack thinks. Parallel skis. She bends nicely. She's wearing a light pink snowsuit that looks great with her dark hair.

Yes, he should feel lucky.

He feels, however, that he would rather be anywhere right now than here. He'd rather be at work. If he really thinks about it. Jack doesn't know what is wrong with him. It's the silence he's missing. Or is it? Is that what it is? Quiet? At work there are noises, people all around him. Talking. Meetings. Maybe it's the fire last night. The fact that he couldn't make it flame brightly.

More likely it's what Rebecca is saying. Nothing. She talks and says nothing. Jack would rather hear the kids on the hill scream *fuck* when they fall.

Yesterday there was a girl on a snowboard. Maybe fifteen. Powder-blue snowsuit. Her blonde hair braided, coming out of her helmet. Jack could tell she was pretty under her goggles and helmet. She came down the hill beside him, then in front of him, and then she fell. She leaned back when she should have leaned forward, and she toppled over in front of him. She called out *fuck* to her friends, right behind her. And Jack passed by quickly, knowing she was okay, and thought to himself that he'd never heard such a pretty word before. *Fuck*. It was full of laughter.

Rebecca is waiting for Jack at the bottom of the hill. She can see him, up top, right at the start of the hill. Just standing there. She thinks, what is he doing? He has no helmet on, not even a hat, although it's cold, and his hair is puffed a bit from the wind. She can see that from all the way down at the bottom. At least he still has hair, Rebecca thinks. She taps her poles on the ground, waiting. She looks around at the sudden influx of kids and parents and teens.

Having slept in, everyone awoke to see the sun and now the hills are full of people. Rebecca thinks of her mother with the kids, thinks of what her mother said to her about how only rich people can ski and how lucky they are to have been married ten years and can take ski vacations. Her mother, the social do-gooder. Volunteers at the YMCA, in the soup kitchen. Her mother wouldn't ever click on ski boots and feel the wind as it hits her face going down the hill. What good is life, Rebecca thinks, if you spend the whole of it worrying about everyone else?

Rebecca knows that's selfish but there are times you want to be selfish. You want to do things for yourself or your family. Not think about everyone else.

Here comes Jack now.

"What were you doing?"

"Just waiting for those other skiers."

Rebecca looks around. There are no other skiers.

"Thinking," Jack shrugs. "We're not racing, right?"

"Right. Nothing is a race." She laughs.

"You don't have to be a bitch about it," Jack says. He gets into the line at the chairlift. Rebecca holds back, astonished.

Bitch? she thinks.

When she is sitting next to him, and two others are with them, Rebecca taps his ski with her pole. She decides not to get angry about the bitch comment. Just like that, Rebecca can now decide not to do something—get angry or sad or go to a party—and she won't do it. That's the beauty of age, she thinks. At some point you say to yourself, enough is enough. No more people-pleasing.

Her mother, however. She can make Rebecca angry.

"I wonder how the kids are doing," Rebecca says suddenly. The two people next to them on the chairlift look over.

Jack nods. "Nice day."

Rebecca smiles.

The others are two teenagers. A girl in grey and black, and a girl in a powder-blue suit. Lovely. Her hair and eyes are complemented by the blue. Her hair is braided and long. She has rosy cheeks. A snowboard. Maybe next year Rebecca will get a blue coat.

The girls look at Rebecca and Jack. Jack knows it's the girl who said *fuck* yesterday. He knows what they are thinking. That he's old. That he's there with his wife who is vomiting up stories about their kids. That he is trying to be young again. He knows they are thinking when they are as old as he is they won't be skiing. They'll be in an old age home. That's what he would have thought when he was their age.

The chairlift stops. Creaks to a halt. Swings.

"Fuck," the girl in blue says.

"Yeah," her friend says.

"Oh my," Rebecca says. Like an old lady, Jack thinks. *Oh my.* When has she ever said that before? She can build a fire. She can ski all day. Why is she saying *oh my*?

Jack looks down and sees a family of four skiing below them. The snow falls off his ski tip and lands quite near the little boy who skis through it, oblivious. In fact, Jack thinks, he could probably spit and the boy would ski through it, not knowing. Family of four. Perfect family. All skiing together. The father laughing proudly. The mother looking snug in her snow pants. Her ass bulging. At least, Jack thinks, Rebecca's ass doesn't bulge.

Why, Rebecca thinks, doesn't Jack talk to her? Only in their room at night. Or in the restaurant after a glass or two of wine. But he doesn't talk to her on the chairlift. It's just occurred to Rebecca that maybe she and Jack are having problems. Real problems. Not just little relationship spats, but real solid problems. Maybe not doing anything as a couple for so many years has really affected them. Maybe they don't know how to be alone together anymore.

Their children are with her mother and father. Probably recycling and eating vegetarian and putting up protest posters and hanging out at the Salvation Army. *Ha*, Rebecca thinks. At least her mother and father have a good relationship. Solid. Her father talks to her mother, at least. They have something to talk about.

Rebecca wonders when Jack stopped talking. She can't remember. And then she wonders when she started talking so much. It was with the kids. When the kids were born she couldn't stop talking. Wanting more attention. Wanting more of Jack's ear. His eyes and his mind were always occupied with the kids. Their freshness, newness, tininess. She wanted some of him.

At work she doesn't talk so much.

Rebecca turns to the powder-blue girl and says, "Do you mind not swinging the chair? It makes me nervous."

The girl's foot stops swinging in the snowboard. "Whatever," she says. Surly.

Jack groans and looks away. The lift starts up again and rushes towards the top of the hill. Getting off, Rebecca is bumped slightly by the snowboarders. At first she doesn't think they meant to do it, snowboarders always seem awkward getting off the lift, but then, when they stop to put their feet in the board, strap themselves in, Rebecca can hear them laughing. Saying, *good one*. Rebecca gathers herself and skis up to them.

And then she does something she never thought she was capable of. She pushes the powder-blue girl over. The girl is standing, waiting for her friend, both her feet in her board. Clipped in. She looks so perfect in her snowsuit, her blonde shining hair in a thick braid, her blue eyes and tinted cheeks. She has strong, long legs. And Rebecca knocks her over and the girl tips in slow motion, and then goes down quickly. Like a domino she knocks into her friend who has just managed to stand up, and soon the two are splayed on the ground in the snow. Rebecca skis past quickly and down the hill. She loses Jack in her haste. In her escape.

Jack helps the girl up, lifts her under her arm and feels the small bulge of her breast with his fingers. He almost drops her he is so astonished and sickened by his fingers. As if they weren't his own. But she doesn't seem to notice and she laughs as she bends now and helps her friend up.

"What a bitch," the girls say. At once. And then they laugh.

Jack laughs and says, "Yep." As if he doesn't even know her, even though the girls know she is his wife, they heard her talking on the lift about their kids. But everyone chooses to ignore this and they head down the hill together and then up the lift together and down again. And Jack talks a bit. And laughs. And finds out the girls can say more than *fuck*. They talk about the terrain park, and which run is the best, and where the jumps should be instead of where they are now, and they talk about the pool at the hotel and that there was a cute guy there last night who, the blue one says, she is sure is in love with the other girl. And they laugh some more.

Down the hill, up the next lift, down again, not thinking about anything but the feel of the hill under her skis. Rebecca spends a lot of time alone. When she sees Jack in the late afternoon, out of the corner of her goggles, he is with the girl in powder blue. He is laughing and talking. She continues on alone.

Jack has a good time and it isn't until his stomach growls that he thinks of Rebecca and wonders where she is and realizes, suddenly, that he hasn't seen her for a long time and it's now way past lunchtime. He looks at his watch. Almost dinnertime.

"Shit," he says. And the girls laugh, because, as Jack realizes again, they think it's funny someone his age knows how to swear.

Jack wonders how his daughter is doing. She is only six and he wonders if she's going to swear when she's fifteen. Of course she is. And snowboard. And talk about guys in pools. He likes most when she leans up next to him on the sofa, if they are watching TV together or reading, when she puts her soft head on his shoulder or his chest and she sighs deeply. Kind of like the sigh Rebecca did earlier on top of the hill. Big sigh. As if she is holding the weight of the world on her shoulders. It's too heavy and she has to lean her head into him for help.

Jack thinks there's something deeper happening here to him. Deeper than mid-life crisis. Than young girls giggling in powder-blue snow suits. Deeper than his wife's incessant talking, than her fire-building abilities, than their wedding anniversary vacation alone. Jack realizes that this deepness has to do with his fear. He's growing older and the rest of the world is staying young. Or it seems that way to him. He's growing older with his wife. And it's almost as if he blames his wife for that. Rebecca feeds him, washes his clothes, makes the bed—can't she control the aging too?

This is ridiculous, Jack thinks. And just then, as he's swooping down the hill, making shortcuts, digging in, Jack sees Rebecca ahead of him, racing towards the finish line. He speeds up, or tries, but ends up with a face full of snow. He has to climb the mountain a bit to get his skis, which have popped off. The two girls pass him giggling.

"Fuck," Jack says.

They laugh louder.

Life, Jack thinks, is so complicated.

Later, Rebecca is nursing a beer, and her ankle, by the fire in the bar of the chalet. Jack finds her there and sits beside her, picks up her leg, under the knee, and rubs her ankle. She tries to smile. His touch is rough and hard. But if she pulls away she doesn't know what will happen.

"Nice fire," Jack says. "Did you make it?"

Rebecca rolls her eyes.

All afternoon she was on the hills alone. She was quiet. She let everyone go ahead of her on the lift so she could sit by herself. So she could look down on the skiers and up to the sky and over the top to the lake that is way down there, frozen over and so white it hurts to open her eyes fully to see it. She thought about nothing. Talked about nothing. Said nothing to anyone. It was good, Rebecca thinks now. To have some peace and quiet. To not have to fill in the blank spots.

"I didn't even know," Rebecca says, finally, after Jack has got himself a beer at the bar and his cheeks become flushed by the fire, "I didn't even know we were fighting."

Jack looks at her. Looks at her small frame, her dark hair and eyes. Her hair is sticking up a bit in the front from wearing her helmet. She is wearing long johns and a turtleneck. A fleece vest. They are sitting before a fire that Rebecca didn't make. Their kids are at home with his mother-in-law and father in-law. They are lucky, Jack thinks. And then he laughs.

"Neither did I," he says. "I didn't know we were fighting either."

"It was a beautiful day, wasn't it?" Rebecca says. She yawns.

"Tomorrow is supposed to be nice too. I asked the guy who runs the ski shop. Sunny. No wind."

"Good," Rebecca says. "No wind. I like no wind."

"Dinner?" Jack says, finishing his beer. He stands. He helps Rebecca stand.

"I might like to go back to the room first," she says. "Fix this hair. Call the kids."

"Don't worry about it," Jack says. "Your hair or the kids."

He takes her hand and leads her into the restaurant. He leads her past the tables with other skiers, with women and men and little kids and teenagers. There are some older couples there. Everyone seems to be smiling. Cheeks are flushed. Wine is being poured. The noise level increases gradually throughout the evening.

In the dark, in their bed, Jack takes Rebecca in his arms. She grimaces when his leg knocks into her ankle. His elbow hits her hip. And then they fit like gloves. Tight together.

"I still don't even know you," Jack whispers, finally, just before Rebecca falls asleep. "I still don't even know myself."

Maybe that's okay, Rebecca thinks. But she doesn't say anything because she's already on her way to sleep.

Drowning

"What are you doing?" Doug sits on the closed lid of the toilet. "Don't we have to hurry?"

Laura is struggling with her pyjama bottoms. She has one foot in and one foot out. She's doing an awkward dance.

"I'm taking a shower."

"You took a shower three hours ago. Before we went to bed."

Laura holds her belly. She feels the contraction, tries to breathe with it, and then lets it go and says, "Damn, damn, damn."

Doug clenches his fists.

"Just help me."

Doug helps Laura into the shower. She is huge. Massive. Like moving a boulder. Her weight is tied up in the tightness in her belly. Doug holds her shoulder as she steps into the tub.

"Shouldn't we call the hospital?"

"I told you. I want to shower."

"I don't want to have the baby here," Doug says. He rubs his eyes. "Really, we should go." Doug thinks about delivering the baby. He shudders. The book says to do it on the kitchen table but Doug thinks the rickety oak table they have wouldn't hold Laura. He imagines getting his hands bloody and the thought makes him feel faint.

"It'll be a while, Doug. Can you reach down to turn the shower on?"

Doug reaches forward and turns the shower on. His hair is sprayed slightly with cold water.

"Jesus, get it warm first," Laura says. She tries to step away from the cold spray but her stomach stays in the mist.

Doug adjusts the temperature.

"Go get dressed," Laura says. "Get everything ready. Pack something to eat."

"Food?" Doug wanders out of the bathroom and down the hall to the kitchen.

"Food?" Laura mimics to herself. "What the hell else?" Her belly is still and quiet beneath her. There is little she can do at the moment. She wills her arms to reach around her back and clean her thighs and ass with the soap. She rinses the shampoo out of her hair. Every eight minutes or so the contractions start again. Laura thinks she can handle them. They feel like period cramps, harder, longer, but easy enough. Breathing. She's trying her breathing. Laura thinks, What's the big deal? Why does everyone make such a big deal out of labour? But then a contraction hits her again and she begins to moan and cry because even if it doesn't hurt as much as she thought it would, it still hurts.

"I'm making peanut butter sandwiches," Doug says. He is standing outside the shower holding a sticky knife in his hand. He licks it.

"I don't think you can take peanut butter into a hospital. Too many people are allergic."

"What? It doesn't say that anywhere in your pregnancy stuff.

No one told you that, did they? And besides," Doug says as he leaves the room again, "if someone had an allergic reaction they'd be fine. They'd be surrounded by doctors and nurses."

Doctors and nurses. Laura bends at the knees to turn off the shower and seizes up. The pain hits her and washes her under. She is under water. She can't breathe.

"Fuck," she shouts.

Doug comes running in from the kitchen. "We have to go," he says. "We have to go now." He can almost see the blood on his hands, the placenta on the floor, a squirming, screaming baby. "Let's go. Now."

When the tightness leaves her body, Laura says, "Help me dry myself." She steps out of the shower and stands unsteadily on her thin legs. Doug dries her, marvelling at how those stick legs can hold up such an enormous package.

"Doug, I don't want to do this," Laura says. Her hands are shaking. Her teeth chatter. "I don't want to go through with this."

Doug stands beside her and wraps her in his arms. "Get dressed," he says. "Everything will be all right."

"You don't understand," Laura says. "I really don't want to do this."

"It'll be over sooner than you think," Doug says. "Besides, you don't want to walk around with that huge stomach for the rest of your life, do you?" He laughs.

Laura limps out of the bathroom and down the hall to their bedroom. She looks at the bed, the sheets thrown off just an hour ago when she first felt the pain deep in her lower back, pushing out through her hips, her belly button.

She can hear Doug in the kitchen. He has the radio on and is washing something in the sink. She thinks she can hear him humming.

"Can't you be quiet?" she shouts. "I'm trying to concentrate."

In the kitchen the noise stops.

Out in the street, trying to remember where they parked the car,

Laura keeps saying, "Really, I don't want to do this," and Doug paces back and forth saying, "Up or down. Did we leave it closer to Markdale Street?"

Laura waits on the front steps while Doug finds the car and drives back to pick her up. The cramps wash over her and take her under but each time Laura rises again and continues to breathe. She is not drowning. She keeps telling herself, "You are not drowning."

Laura suddenly notices the tulip in the dark of the garden. A dark red bud, close to opening. She stares at it.

"Come on. Get in," Doug says. He comes over to help her up. Laura stares at the tulip.

"Look," she says. "It's about to open."

"Just in time for the baby," Doug says.

"I'm not going through with this."

"Get in the car," Doug says.

Laura stands. She lowers her knees and reaches to pick the tulip. She breaks it in half. "You can't tell me what to do." She straightens her back, feels a crack somewhere in her spine, something shifting, and then she hobbles up the steps and back into the apartment building.

"Where are you going?"

"I'm getting out of here."

"Laura."

"I told you. This isn't going to happen to me."

"Jesus Christ."

The door shuts behind Laura, and Doug stands in the road with his hands hanging at his sides. He tastes peanut butter in his teeth. He walks up to the door and tries to open it. It is locked. He fumbles in his pockets for the keys.

Laura takes the stairs up to their second-floor apartment. The contractions are closer together and she is so angry that she wills them to hurt her. They do and she buckles over several times, almost falling.

"I'm not doing this, I'm not doing this, I'm not doing this."

Laura opens the door of their apartment and moves over to sit on the sofa. Suddenly a gush of hot water—hot, Laura thinks, it's so hot—leaks down her legs. She decides not to sit on the sofa. She decides to sit on the kitchen floor.

Doug enters the apartment. He rushes over to where Laura is sitting. He slips in the puddle of water, but rights himself awkwardly.

"What's going on?" he shouts. "You're having a baby. You're having our baby. Go. Go. Go." He moves his hands as if he's shooing away a cat.

Laura laughs.

"What's on the floor? What spilled?"

"My water."

"What water—oh, shit." Doug kneels beside Laura. "Tell me what's going on, Laura. I can't deliver a baby. I can't do it."

"You don't have to deliver it," Laura says. "I'm not having a baby. I'm just going to sit here and rest until the pain stops. I'm not having a baby."

"What the hell are you talking about?" Doug collapses beside Laura. He rests his back on the kitchen cupboards.

"There is nothing inside of me," Laura says. "There can't be anything inside of me. Right?"

Doug stares coldly at his wife. "You've been eating right, you quit smoking, you stopped drinking, you did prenatal exercises, for nine months—nine months!—and now you're telling me that there is nothing in your womb? Look at you. You're huge. We had an ultrasound. We have a picture." Doug jumps up and grabs the ultrasound picture from the front of the fridge, stuck there since Laura was eighteen weeks pregnant, stuck there with a magnet of a little Rastafarian man holding a surfboard that reads BARBADOS, and he sits down again with it, "Our baby. A picture of it. Look."

Laura looks at the picture. She can barely make out the tiny body, the large head. But there, centre picture, is a little hand. Five fingers. She can see them. Those small fingers, an X-ray of the bones. She wills herself not to see them.

"I'm not going anywhere."

"Laura, please." Doug stands up. "I'm calling an ambulance. They'll take you to the hospital in a straitjacket."

"You won't call an ambulance."

"Why not?"

"Because they cost money and you're cheap."

"Why do they cost money?"

"One hundred dollars, I think. Maybe two hundred. If it's not a life-or-death emergency."

"This is both," Doug says. "Life and death. I'll die if I have to bring life into this kitchen myself."

Laura laughs. "Keep making jokes," she says, "you're taking the pain away."

"Oh, Laura, honey. Laura." Doug sits next to her again. "Honey. Laura." He smoothes her dirty blonde hair and notices the sweat on her brow. "We're having a baby. We've been waiting for this. Honey."

"Don't sweet-talk me."

"Come on." Doug's voice is smooth and soft. "Let's go have our baby. We're going to be a family now."

"I don't want a baby, I don't want to be a family. I've just decided that this was a bad idea."

"Oh, man."

They wait while a wave of pain takes Laura under again. She holds Doug's hand. Squeezes so hard he feels his bones are breaking. He figures if he drives very fast and rushes through every light then they will get there in time. He tries to help Laura up but she remains steadfastly stuck to the floor. The water pools around her. Each time she has a contraction more hot water pushes out.

"We're not ready for a baby," Laura says. "We fight all the time."

"We don't fight."

"Yes we do."

"No we don't."

"See."

Doug stares at the wall, willing himself not to say anything. "We don't, and besides, all couples fight."

"No they don't."

"Yes they do."

"Not couples who are having babies. You can't fight in front of a baby."

"Why not? It's good for children to see parents disagreeing, to know you don't resolve fights with violence or long-standing anger, to know that you can talk things out."

"We don't talk things out. And we swear too much. I say *fuck* a lot. You swear."

"No I don't. Not really." Doug runs his fingers through his hair.

They sit in silence. Laura stares at the water around them. Doug stares at Laura's stomach.

"I'm scared," Doug says.

"You're scared?"

"Yes. I want to go to the hospital. Now."

Laura bites her lower lip. She fights the tightening in her belly. The severe cramping, her muscles pulling together, gripping like clamps pulled tight.

"Oh, God," she moans.

Doug crouches next to Laura. He holds her head against his chest. She struggles to get free.

"Don't touch, don't touch." Her breathing is random and fluttery, uncontrolled. "Don't touch."

Doug stands and walks over to the phone. He avoids the water on the floor. He picks up the phone.

"We don't even have a house," Laura pants. "We live in a crappy apartment in a bad part of the city. Where will our child go to school?"

"We'll move before the baby is old enough to go to school," Doug says. He puts the phone down again. "We'll both get jobs again, you'll see."

"I have a job," Laura says. "I'm on maternity leave, remember? It's you who doesn't have a job."

"I've been looking."

"No you haven't."

Doug thinks about how he sits with the paper spread out in front of him every day, a pen in hand, a cup of cooling coffee beside him. He reads the classifieds, he reads the sports, he reads the front page. He watches the weather channel and sometimes catches a ball game on TV.

Laura struggles from the floor.

"You wanted this baby too," Doug says. "You're the one—"

"I'm the one what? I'm the one who forced you to do it? No, Doug. You're the one. You lost your job. You lost your job and wanted something meaningful in your life. You lost your goddamn job because you are lazy and kept calling in sick, because you'd lie home all day in front of the TV."

"I was sick."

"No you weren't."

"I didn't like my job."

"Jesus," Laura moans. She is standing before the sink, her fingers hooked into the handles of the cabinets above. She is bent forward, stretching her back. "Help me."

Doug moves towards her, tries to remember what he learned in class, tries to remember what to do. "Nine months," he mumbles. "We had nine months to talk about all this and you're bringing it up now?" He touches her back.

"Don't touch me."

Doug suddenly remembers the video they watched in the birthing class they attended. There was a husband who asked questions. "Do you want me to rub your back?" "Do you want some water?" "Do you feel all right?" At the end of the class all the mothers, when asked what they thought about the video—about the smiling, happy woman who answered her husband kindly, took care of him, of his anxiety—the women, every single one of them, including Laura, said they would have shot the husband. Laura said that if Doug asked her one stupid question when she was in pain she would punch him in the face.

Doug stands helplessly behind Laura, in the water on the floor, and he says nothing.

"Stop it," Laura says. "I want you to stop it, Doug. If you do one thing in your life, stop this baby from coming. Not now. I'm not ready now."

"You have no choice in the matter, Laura." Doug walks to the phone again and dials 911.

"Hello? Can I order an ambulance?"

"You can't order an ambulance," Laura groans.

"My wife's having a baby." After a pause, Doug adds, "No, I can't take her to the hospital." He pauses again. "Why?" Doug looks at Laura. "She won't let me, that's why."

"Hang up. Hang up right now." Laura tries to walk over to the phone but finds her legs aren't working. She is rooted to the spot she's standing. "Jesus, Jesus, Jesus." She starts to shake. "What am I going to do?" she cries.

"Have the baby," Doug whispers. "Have the baby and then we'll get on with our lives."

Laura's legs suddenly give out and she crumples to the floor. Doug drops the phone and goes to her. He crouches.

"I love you," he whispers. "I love you."

"I'm holding this baby in," Laura whimpers. "I'll keep my legs crossed. I'm holding this baby in until you get a job." And then Laura starts to laugh. She can't stop. Wave after wave after wave hits her until she goes under for too long and can't get back up. "I'm drowning," she says. She is floating somewhere beneath the sea, lying on her kitchen floor, Doug kneeling beside her. He is crying.

"Help," he shouts. "Somebody help me."

Making Spirits Bright

They are down south and it's hot and the little kid is digging in the sand. He is singing "Here comes Santa Claus." He looks up from his hole. He looks up from where the water is streaming into his hole in the sand and he says, "How's it go again, Mommy? What comes next?"

"Something about his reindeers," the mommy yawns. She is sitting on a lounge chair in the sun. Her leather skin is everywhere, pushing out of her bikini, her blonde hair almost translucent. She is painting her nails fire-engine red.

"Something about Mrs. Claus, maybe?" the mommy says logically. "Maybe something more about the lane where he lives?"

"No," shouts the dad. He is back a bit, in the shade of a beach umbrella, his arms and legs covered. His feet are bare, though, and later, when he's getting ready for the Christmas Eve Dinner Dance in the hotel, he won't be able to put socks on over his burned and peeling skin. "Reindeers. It's definitely reindeers."

It's the first holiday the mommy's been on since she had the little boy. The first holiday in the sun. They went skiing last year but the little boy was three then and afraid of the snow so she sat with him in the lodge while the father went up and down the slopes all day and sat in the bar all night. The mommy has a tanning bed at home, though, so thankfully she looks like she's always on holiday. The little boy has become an expert at shutting the giant roof of the bed over his mother and then playing quietly on the floor while she lies still and lets the tanning lights do their trick. At the grocery store the women all say, "Where've you been this time? You're always going somewhere."

It's Christmas Eve and the beach is deserted. The little boy moves sand with a shovel into the hole he's dug. The mommy looks up. She can't believe it. Her boy digs and digs a hole, working so carefully for so long, and then he fills it up and starts again. She can't believe it. The mommy doesn't understand her little boy any more than she understands her husband. The dad sits under that beach umbrella a little distance away from them and he watches them all day long. He doesn't offer to help the boy dig or fill, and he doesn't read a book or do a crossword puzzle. He sits and watches and waits. But waits for what, the mommy cannot tell. And it doesn't matter, really, that she doesn't understand her boy. But it matters quite a bit that she doesn't understand the dad.

"Nixon and Blixen," the dad shouts. "That's how it goes."

"Nixon? Sweetie, not Nixon," the mommy says. She giggles. "Vixen?"

The little boy starts singing again, "Nixon and Blixen and all the reindeers dancing on the lane."

"That's right, pumpkin!" The mommy smiles. "That's just about right! What a smart boy I have."

"He learned it in school," the dad shouts. "They must have taught that to him in school."

The mommy sighs. Every day back home she takes the little boy to school in the mornings and then picks him up at lunch. He spends the afternoon with her. He plays. She tans. Sometimes they bake cookies. What does he know about what the little boy does in school? What does the dad know about it?

"I'm hungry," the little boy says. "All this singing and digging makes me hungry."

The mommy tries to pull a bag of carrots from her beach bag but her nails are still wet and so she picks up the beach bag with her toe and tosses it towards the boy. It lands in his new hole.

"It's wet, it's wet," the dad shouts. "Get it out."

The mommy sighs and rises from her chair. She gingerly plucks the bag from the hole and opens it. She takes out some carrots.

"I don't want carrots," the little boy says. "I hate carrots."

The water is so blue and shimmering that the glare hurts the mommy's eyes. She shades her eyes with her hands, her fresh-painted fingernails shining brightly. He's four years old, she says to herself. "There are cookies in the bottom of the bag, honey. If you can find them you can have them." The little boy dives towards the beach bag.

"He'll ruin his dinner," the dad shouts. At dinner the little boy will sit before his plate of roast beef and look at it. He'll look at it until he swears he can see it move. He'll swear he can see the creepy-crawlies moving on it, the flies and gnats from the dessert table, there, on his roast beef. Then he'll cry and scream and his mommy will have to take him back to their room and she'll sit in front of the TV and miss watching her husband try to dance on his burned, sockless feet at the Christmas Eve Dinner Dance.

The little boy eats the cookies. Occasionally he looks at his dad while he's chewing. The dad looks at him.

The mommy turns towards the dad. "I'm going for a swim," she says. "It's hot."

The dad nods.

"Will you watch him?"

"Sure," the dad says. "Sure I'll watch him." The dad puts his eyes on the little boy and doesn't take them off. He stares at the little boy until he is sure he can see right through him and to the water and to his wife, swimming in the water, her leather-skin looking somehow healthy when it's wet, and then past her to the end of the horizon where he stares and stares, looking right through the body and bones of his son.

The mommy swims.

The little boy digs.

The mommy's hair flows out behind her in the water. She can feel it around her shoulders, around her neck. Later, after the little boy is in bed, after his screaming fit in the restaurant, after they've watched a bit of TV and the mommy wonders where the dad is, the mommy will take a bath and she'll remember when her hair flowed out behind her in the sea.

"Are you sure he comes here?" the little boy says quietly.

"What?" the dad shouts.

"Santa Claus, are you sure he comes here?"

"To the beach?"

"No, to the hotel."

"Yes, I'm sure. I've told you a million times. He'll come here."

"But there's no fireplace."

"Speak up, boy."

"There's no fireplace."

"He can walk through the door," the dad shouts. "He can walk straight through it without hurting himself. Don't be ridiculous. He doesn't need a fireplace."

"But there's no tree."

"What?"

"There's no tree."

"What are you shouting about?" the mommy shouts from the water. "You're both shouting."

"He doesn't need a tree. He can put the presents on the floor. He puts them on the floor under the tree, doesn't he? Well, doesn't he?"

"On the floor?" the little boy asks.

"What?"

The mommy comes quickly out of the water. "What's wrong?" she asks. "Why are you shouting?"

"The boy thinks that Santa won't come," the dad says.

"He'll come," the mommy says, bending down and touching her little boy's head. "He told me he would. In the mall, last Tuesday, when I was buying this nail polish"—she holds out her fingers—"he told me himself he'd come down here and give you presents."

"Oh," the little boy says. Not for a minute does he believe that the Santa in the mall is the one who can walk through doors. The boy continues to sing.

"What about 'Jingle Bells'?" the dad shouts. "I'm sick of that lane song. Where would Santa have a lane? The North Pole? The North Pole has no lanes. Just snow. Right?"

"Why don't you come over here?" the mommy says. "Why are you shouting so much?"

The dad puts his hands up to his temples. He massages them. This is the look he likes when he is tired of the mommy and her ways, when he is tired of her leather skin, of the white-blonde hair, of the way she calls the little boy by pet names, honey and bunny and poopsy and pumpkin. He rubs his temples. The dad also uses this look when he's at especially important meetings with especially important clients and when they are discussing especially important things. This happens often. And later, down at the beach, after the Christmas Eve Dinner Dance at the hotel, when he's hobbling around on his burned feet in the sand with his voluptuous dance partner, the dad will use this look again. He'll use it to impress her and she'll like it and she'll say, "Oh, do you have a headache? You poor man," and she'll touch his hands which are touching his temples and his feet won't hurt anymore. The mommy will float in her bathtub with her hair streaming out and she'll think about the sea she can hear through the open window. The waves crashing against the sand. And the little boy will lie in bed at just about this time, willing Santa Claus to melt through his door and take him away. Take him back home. Where there's a tree and a fireplace. He is sure Santa doesn't put the presents on the floor, but he can't remember last year. Last year he was only three.

"Here comes jingle bells, here comes jingle bells," the little boy sings.

"No, no, no, no, no."

"He can sing it just about any way he wants to sing it, can't you, poopsy?" the mommy says.

"Doesn't he learn anything at that school? What do they teach him there?"

The little boy continues to dig.

The mommy sits back down on her chair. Her wet skin glistens. The dad massages his temples.

"You know," the mommy begins. "If you would just—"

"Don't you start with me," the dad shouts. "Don't start."

"Dashing through the snow," the little boy sings loudly. Very loudly. He sings it so loudly that he drowns out the dad and the mommy. He drowns out the sea and the waves crashing and the gulls swooping wildly in the air. He drowns out the sun even and everything seems dark suddenly. "On a one-horse open sleigh."

"Well," the dad says. "You know that one, don't you? You know that one well. I told you they taught him something in that school. I told you he was learning something."

"Merry Christmas," the mommy says. She scoops up some sand, willing it to stick to her fingernail polish. But the fingernail polish is dry, it's been dry for a while, and so the sand rolls off the glossy red paint and into her lap.

Much later, after the dad comes back from his walk with his dance partner, after the mommy has had her nice, soothing bath, after the little boy has fallen asleep on the floor, propped up beside the door and after all is done and not said, then the presents will be laid on the floor in a haphazard pile and the stockings will be rested against a chair leg and someone big and jolly will slowly make his way through the door and out into the night. The dad will nestle tight next to the mommy in bed, both of them listening to the little boy's breathing coming snore-like through the hotel walls and into their room.

"Merry Christmas to you too," the dad shouts now at the mommy.

"O'er the fields we go," the little boy sings, "laughing all the way. Ha. Ha. Ha. Bells on cocktails ring, making spirits bright...."

"Cocktails?" the mommy interrupts. She giggles. "Oh, bunny, that's perfect. What a perfectly lovely idea."

The dad laughs.

The family packs up their belongings and moves sluggishly through the sand together towards their hotel. The little boy rests his hand in his mother's and she wraps her fire-engine red nails around his palm. The dad carries the shovel and bucket and beach bag. His feet are stinging. They are feeling tender.

"Cocktails," the mommy murmurs. "What a perfectly lovely idea."

Christmas Has Gone to the Dogs

She says he hasn't been breathing well for about nine hours. She says he's been raspy. She says his breathing isn't deep. Like maybe he's got something jammed in his throat or maybe his throat is closing up slowly or maybe he's just tired of breathing deep and is doing all this to bother her.

It's Christmas Eve, she tells me. As if that should explain everything.

I tell her to go sit in the waiting room and the doctor will look at him. I tell her to wheel him in but he keeps falling out of the wheelchair and, when I go to help, his cowboy boots with the big pointy toes poke me in the thigh. I know I'll go home tomorrow to Dwayne and he'll say, "W-where'd you get those bruises?" He'll tap me on the shoulder and say, "T-this is why you should quit your job. It was Christmas Eve last night and you've got bruises on your thighs."

She keeps apologizing for his boots, saying that they were the only pair she could find in the closet that didn't have crap on them. She says that all his boots are covered in crap from being out in the pen with the dogs.

I don't really care what she is saying because it's 11 p.m. and I've been here forever. Because in about eight hours my daughter will be up waiting for me to get home so she can open her presents. My patience is limited. Especially for a doped-up cowboy and his girl.

"Drag him in if you have to," I say to her. I drop him because I'm carrying him under his armpits and the smell just hit my nose. "Jesus, he stinks. I'm not touching him."

"It's the dogs," the woman explains. "Have a little sympathy." She takes him by his cowboy boots and she starts pulling him into the waiting room towards the little play castle for the sick kids.

Dwayne's always wanting me to quit this job but what would we eat for dinner? Where would we live? Sitting there on the couch every day watching TV, checking on his bets at the track, not even attempting to get a job. Not even making sure our daughter does her homework.

"Air," Dwayne says, when he's being funny. "We'll eat air."

I rub my thigh where the point of the boot stuck in. Big bruise. I can feel it. Wonder for a moment if I can file for workers' compensation. Last week Della got a scalpel stuck in her hand and she got six weeks' full pay. Some nights I want to stick a scalpel in my hand just to see what I'll get. Hepatitis, no doubt.

I didn't go through two years of nursing college to sit behind this desk in Emergency on Christmas Eve and stare at the drunks in the waiting room. I didn't take student loans to pick shallow-breathing men off the floor.

"Have you got a Kleenex?"

The woman is back. She's got her face close to mine, pushing her pink lips into my cubbyhole. I see that the cowboy has fallen again and the woman has left him lying on the floor. He's spread out, arms stretched their fullest, legs together, and he reminds me of something, but I don't know what.

"Travis needs a Kleenex."

"He told you that, did he?"

"He didn't have to tell me that. Look at him."

There's blood on his upper lip, dripping down from his nose.

"Do you think he broke it?"

I shrug. "Won't help with the breathing, though."

"Yes, I suppose."

The woman takes the Kleenex and I notice her fingernails. Just like mine. Glue-ons with big candy hearts painted in the middle. She chose white nail polish, I chose green for Christmas.

"Hey," I say.

She looks at my nails. She smiles. She goes back to her raspy man and dabs at his upper lip. She bends down to where he is on the floor and I can see the top of her undies poking out of her tight blue jeans. Little pink hearts on those too. The woman is loaded with hearts. Seems sad to me that a woman who spends time and thought on her appearance ends up with a stinky man like that.

The doctor comes in from outside where he's been smoking. He's a new one. Young and tired-looking and fed up with the hours.

"What have we got?" he asks. "Jesus on the cross?"

"That's what he looks like," I say. "I knew he reminded me of something."

"That's the problem with Christmas," the doctor says. "It's just a commercial holiday these days. Nobody remembers how it started."

"That's a problem?" I say.

He shrugs.

"You shouldn't smoke."

"Don't you think I know that?" he says.

"That gum works if you chew all the time."

"Tried it. Didn't work. Besides, what would people give me for Christmas if they couldn't give me cigarettes?"

"What about the patch? Have you tried the patch?"

The doctor nods in the direction of the man and woman in the waiting room. "What's this all about?"

"Oh, he can't breathe."

"Drug overdose?"

I shrug. "You're the doctor."

"Should we put him on oxygen? What happened to his nose?"

"Listen," I say. "You're the doctor. You tell me what to do. That's how this works."

The doctor looks nervous. All his decisions are based on nervousness. He looks as if he'd jump out of his skin if you poked him just a little.

"You know," I say. "I'd check him out first before you struggle with the mask. I'd wheel him into the room and see where he's at. Just a suggestion."

"Good idea." The doctor goes into the waiting room and talks to the man. He bends down to talk to him and then he reels back from the smell. "Jesus," I hear him say. "He stinks."

"It's the dogs," the woman says to me after they struggle the man up from the floor and begin to wheel him into the treatment room. "They piss on his pant legs all the time."

I nod. Easy to see that happening.

"You try vinegar?" I say. I'm feeling some sort of holiday spirit towards her because of our shared nails.

She shakes her head.

"Vinegar takes the smell out of everything."

"Puts a new smell in, I suppose," she says.

"I suppose."

They wheel past me and into the treatment room. I can hear the doctor struggling with the man, loading him onto the table. I can hear the doctor gagging a bit at the smell. He asks the woman to grab hold of the man's legs. She's easygoing. She helps out.

"Frosty the Snowman" is playing on the hospital speaker system.

"Can you hear me?" the doctor asks, loudly. "Can you hear me, Mr. Martel?"

"He don't like to be called Mr. Martel," the woman says. She sounds bored. I bet anything she's picking at those hearts on her nails and thinking about what she'd like to eat for breakfast. I've been there. I want to shout, *Don't waste your nails. Keep them pretty for the holidays.*

"Travis," the doctor hollers. "Can you hear me, Travis? What seems to be the problem?"

"He's not deaf," the woman says. "He can't breathe."

"Nine hours," the doctor says. "Why'd you wait so long? He can't even open his eyes."

"You're going to blame *me*? You're blaming me? It's Christmas Eve and you're blaming me?"

The woman comes out of the treatment room and settles down in the chair before my desk as if we're sisters together in this.

"He's going to blame me," she says, nodding.

I nod back. What else can I do? It's 11:30 now and I have another eight hours and a bit until my shift is over. I'm thinking about Tina, my daughter, and whether or not she'll like the new CD I got her. It was on her wish list but she changes her mind so much these days I never can be sure.

There's no one else in the waiting room.

"So, you get your nails done at the mall?" she asks.

"Uh-huh."

"And you went for the hearts because they're on special?"

"Because I liked them."

"But they were on special last week."

"That's right. Didn't hurt my bank account."

"I hear you," the woman says.

"You have to try to breathe, Mr. Martel," the doctor shouts. "Just try."

"He hates that," the woman tells me. She sits back in the chair. She looks like she'd like to put her feet on my desk. "He hates being called Mr. Martel. It reminds him of his dad. He hated his dad."

"I know where he's coming from," I say and then I regret saying it. This woman doesn't have to know about me. But the woman ignores the comment. I look into my computer, pretending to be busy.

"What's it like working here?" the woman asks. "I been thinking about getting a new job. The dogs are getting too much for me."

"You can't just get a job here," I say. "You have to go to school."

"I went to school."

We look at each other.

"Okay, Mr. Martel," the doctor says. "Where'd your wife go?"

"He's not my husband," the woman says to me.

"I'm going to have to put an oxygen mask on you," the doctor shouts. "Just hold still."

"Oh," the woman laughs. "He'll fight that one."

"He's too weak to fight."

"Not Travis. He's never too weak to throw a good punch." She chuckles. She starts picking under her nails with a pencil she found on my desk. "You know, there are times I would just like to open all the pens and let the dogs out into the wild. Let them run away. I feel this way especially around the holidays. They need to run, you know."

"You got a farm?" I yawn.

"More like a mill," she whispers. "About a hundred of them die a year."

I sit up. "Puppies?"

"Big dogs too."

"That's sick."

The woman looks offended. "We have to make money somehow."

"By killing dogs?"

The woman stands and walks into the waiting room. She stands in front of the castle.

"Bet this is covered in germs," the woman says. More to herself than to me.

I like puppies. Dwayne and Tina, they'd get a cat if we had the money. But I'm more a dog person. My dad had dogs on the farm but they were treated like wildlife. Slept and ate in the barn. Ate scraps. Like pigs, almost. My dad would take them hunting.

"Nurse," the doctor shouts. "Help me."

I sigh. I go into the room where Travis lies on the table, his big damn boots messing up the wall, making black scrapes in the wallpaper. He's struggling with the doctor, fighting him off. The doctor is leaning over Travis, trying to force the mask on the man's face.

"Let me do it," I sigh. "This is what I went to school for."

The doctor doesn't argue. He hands me the mask.

"In the spirit of Christmas and all," he says as if he's doing me a favour.

Travis looks at me. His beady eyes open. I see the puppies dying and I think, *Bastard, I should let you suffocate.* But I put the mask on him. No problem. He trusts a woman. He likes my nails. Gives me an approving glance. He breathes a little easier but I can hear a wheezing in his lungs.

"What are you going to do with him?"

The doctor shrugs. He rubs his eyes. "I don't know. I can't think. I've been on call for seventy-two hours."

The doctor looks like he's going to cry and this makes me impatient. I don't want to stay here a minute longer than I have to. I'm not going to sit in the coffee shop comforting a new doctor who's too tired to know right from wrong.

"Okay, let's see." I lift the man's head. His eyes are closed again. His breathing is too shallow.

"It's those dogs." The woman is standing behind me. She is breathing on my neck. I feel her sharp nails on my shoulder.

"What do you mean?" the doctor asks.

"He puffs up when he's around them."

"Allergies?"

The woman shrugs. "I don't know, I'm not the doctor around here."

"Listen," the doctor shouts. "Listen to me." But when we stop and turn to look at him he says nothing.

"Anyway," the woman continues, "those dogs come close to Travis and he starts sniffling like there's no tomorrow. I think it's the dogs."

"Why would he work with them then?" I ask.

"I need antihistamines," the doctor says, and I leave the room and head down to the medicine cabinet. I take my key out of my pocket and open the door. But when I come back to the room the doctor and the woman ignore me. They are both staring hard at Travis. He is waving his hands in the air like he's conducting an orchestra or waving down a jumbo jet. His breathing has stopped.

"Do something," I say.

But no one moves.

"I really want to get out of the dog business," the woman whispers. "I don't like those stupid dogs. They smell. And the work. It's crazy."

I rush to the oxygen tank. I turn it up. I inject the antihistamine but the man's arms shoot straight out and then flap down at his sides and I know, suddenly, that he's dead.

"Nine hours," the doctor says. "Couldn't you have brought him in earlier?"

"He didn't want to come. It was dinner for the dogs and then there was a Christmas special on TV." The woman is staring at Travis. She is still. Every inch of her is on edge. I can see the veins in her neck bulging. Her long nails dig into the palms of her hands.

I hear bells at the Emergency door. The annual arrival of Santa Claus for the staff.

The doctor hasn't moved an inch. He's wound up so tight that he's going to explode.

"Boo," I shout.

It is Christmas. The doctor and the woman both jump. They jump so high and they scream so loud that I think they could wake the dead.

But they don't.

Travis lies there with his cowboy boots on and a smell that could knock the air out of you.

It amazes me, sometimes, what we do for money.

The Cat

Nigel unclips his seat belt and gets out of the car. He moves quickly into the headlights and bends down, staring at the wet pavement in front of him.

"Oh no," he whispers.

The cat lies, motionless, before him.

The rain pours down.

"Hurry up," Beth shouts from the open window. "I'm in a lot of pain, Nigel, hurry up."

"Just a minute," Nigel says. "Oh shit." The cat lies there on the road, legs stiff. Nigel wipes the palms of his hands on his jeans. His hair is wet with rain. He rubs a hand across his eyes.

Suddenly the cat leaps up, turns quickly around, looks at Nigel and then runs into the bushes. Nigel is astonished. He stands up, scours the bushes for a minute and then, when he is satisfied the cat has disappeared, he climbs back into the car.

"A cat," he says to Beth. "It was a cat. I hit a cat."

"I'm in pain, you know. I'm in a lot of pain." Beth touches her left ankle gingerly. "You have no right to just get out of the car, to *stop* the car, and try and save some dumb animal. I'm the one who needs help, Nigel. Damnit."

"It took off," Nigel says. "It was unconscious but then it took off."

Beth sucks in her breath. "Let's just go," she groans. "Let's just get going." She is talking through her teeth. "I'm swelling up. I need some painkillers."

Nigel is driving Beth to the hospital. It is late in the evening. Beth has sprained her ankle. The ankle is swollen but Beth is afraid to look. She sprained her ankle while running into the cottage from the boathouse to answer the phone. They are in the country. Nigel thinks he knows the way to the hospital. He was there once when he was a kid and he stepped on a rusty nail on the dock. His father drove him to the hospital and he remembers waiting in the Emergency room and the nurse buying him a hot chocolate. They have been driving for fifteen minutes. Beth is cursing and complaining beside him.

When they get to the hospital Nigel pays the parking attendant and then wheels a chair to the car and helps Beth into Emergency. She is groaning and carrying on. Nigel sprained his ankle once but he doesn't remember it being this painful. He helps Beth as much as he can. There is one nurse behind the desk. She is watching TV. Nigel rings the bell to get her attention, fills out the forms and watches as a young man wheels Beth into the X-ray room.

"I don't need an x-ray," Beth argues. "I know it's sprained. I'm not an idiot. I can tell when something's sprained."

Nigel settles down in front of the TV. It is quiet in the hospital. There is no one else in Emergency. He feels calm suddenly. The cat ran away. Beth is being looked after. And he's far from his father's cottage, the cottage with the memories he is trying to keep golden, the memories Beth is destroying, taking down, bit by bit, sucking away from him. She is creating a new set of memories, a bitter, arguing, nattering, painful set of memories.

The rain pelts down outside, pattering gently on the windows. Unlike the TV at the cottage, this one has cable and so Nigel can watch whatever he wants without having to adjust an antenna, without Beth standing inside shouting to him outside, to *turn it this way, turn it that way, can't you do something right for once?* He looks around for the remote control and then spots it in the nurse's hand. The nurse smiles nicely at Nigel and then changes the channel to a program called *When Animals Attack*. Nigel sighs. He'd much rather be watching the baseball game but instead he watches a rhinoceros maul a photographer at an African Lion Safari Park in Dallas, Texas. The photographer bleeds from his arm, his stomach and his leg. He runs around in circles with his hands covering his ears, screaming. Nigel feels nothing for this man. He's been to so many hospitals and seen so much pain and blood in the last two months that he feels desensitized to human emotion.

That's why the cat shocked him, he thinks. Animal pain. Something hard to pin down, hard to evaluate, hard to control. Nigel has no idea if the cat is all right. It could say nothing. It didn't whine or complain. It just looked at him and then jumped up and ran into the bushes.

Beth insisted on running to answer the phone. It was raining and the walkway was slippery. There was someone she wanted to speak to, she said, an old friend, someone other than Nigel. Two weeks in the country in a ratty old cottage with Nigel, she said, was almost unbearable— there must be someone calling who could take her mind off the boredom. There must be someone who would have something interesting to say. She slipped on the stone walkway Nigel's father was so proud of and lay there on the hard path, getting wet in the rain, screaming for somebody to put her out of her misery, for someone to take the pain away. The phone rang on and on. Nigel thought the phone rang on for quite a considerable time before it stopped. He thought about this later. He thought about this when he was driving and Beth was complaining, just before he hit the cat. Who would let a phone ring for so long? The thought bothered him.

They have been married two months now and Beth has already received three stitches in a finger from cutting potatoes for the grill, suffered a minor concussion from walking into a door at the mall, and severely bruised (and then lost) a toenail while dancing. And now this—a sprained ankle from running for the phone. Nigel would like to be sympathetic but it's hard to feel anything when these accidents are occurring all the time.

He wonders what happened to that cat.

"Coffee?" The nurse sits down next to Nigel and hands him a Styrofoam cup.

"Yes, thanks."

"Don't worry, honey. Your friend will be fine."

Friend, Nigel thinks. Friend. He sips his coffee. If only they were friends. If only they had that in common.

"You don't need to cry anymore."

"Pardon me?"

The nurse points to Nigel's face. Nigel stands and looks at his reflection in the pop machine window. There is dirt and grime washed with rainwater streaking down his face.

"I hit a cat," he says. "I hit a cat on the road. It's raining out there. Pretty badly."

"Oh dear." The nurse looks concerned and amused at the same time. Nigel thinks about how much roadkill this nurse must see on the highways and realizes that one dead cat isn't anything to get worked up about in the country.

He married Beth two months ago and everything changed so quickly. One day she was his beautiful fiancée, happy, laughing all the time, eager to please, the next day, after a little cake, some champagne and a minister's blessing, she was a holy terror, a complaining, unhappy woman. She said, *tough*, she said, *marriage will do that to you.* She said she didn't know how hard it would be, being married, how everyone looked at you differently, how life turned right upside down and inside out and nothing, not anything, would ever be the same anymore.

"Up here for a holiday?" the nurse asks. She sips her coffee. She mutes the TV.

"We just needed to get away," Nigel says. "Away from the city. We needed to talk."

"Ah, yes." The nurse shakes her head up and down and then back and forth. "The city." She hums a bit.

"Have you ever heard of a cat being knocked unconscious and then getting up and running off into the bushes?" Nigel uses a Kleenex and his spit to wipe the streaked dirt off his face. He stares at his reflection in the pop machine.

"Oh, all the time," the nurse says. "They run off to die." She looks at Nigel's face as it falls. "I mean, sometimes they do that. Sometimes they are fine. They're usually hearty animals, cats. I have six of them. Barn cats, of course, but six." The nurse nods her head up and down. "Good mousers."

Nigel looks at his watch. It is late. He sits down again next to the nurse. He wonders where the time goes when it passes and he thinks about how each second ticks out the rest of your life.

"She'll be a while yet," the nurse says. "X-ray, painkillers, wrapping it up."

The nurse leans back in the plastic, moulded hospital chair and watches TV with Nigel. They watch a boa constrictor attack an exotic dancer. There really isn't much movement. The woman is dancing, then she slows down a bit, then she stops. Her face turns red. The audience claps nervously. Her face becomes even redder. She collapses on the stage. The snake looks the same. It is wrapped around her body and it stays wrapped, there is no movement in the snake. The woman passes out and several men in the audience jump up and climb onto the stage. The nurse uses the remote control to turn up the volume on the TV so they can hear what happened.

There are eyewitness accounts, and then the rescued dancer in the hospital, and finally the host promising more to come. Nigel shakes his head. He is always astonished with what he can see on TV.

What was a cat doing in the middle of nowhere?

Why did the phone keep ringing and ringing and ringing and ringing?

Nigel had spent summers at the cottage until he was fifteen. His father built it and he helped as much as a fifteen-year-old could; when his hormones weren't raging, when he wasn't drawn to the dock with the girls in their bikinis and the cool, cool water. He would finish school for the year, pack his shorts and swim trunks and meet his father at the subway station close to the highway. Nigel's mother stayed in the city, working. When his parents divorced, the routine continued. Nothing changed.

Nigel's father died last year after a lengthy illness. He left him the cottage and the lake and the trees. He left him the memories of a more peaceful time, memories of childhood, when everything was innocent and wonderful. There was no pain back then. Not really. Nothing that stopped Nigel in his tracks, made him blink or turn around.

Nigel sighs. He's getting awfully sick of hospital waiting rooms and Styrofoam coffee cups.

"It's okay, honey," the nurse says. "The dancer survived. Look, there she is in the hospital."

Nigel smiles. "But what about the snake?"

The nurse laughs.

It is getting later and later. The sky is black and the rain comes down hard.

A young girl walks into the Emergency room and rings the bell for the nurse. Nigel looks towards the door. He wonders where her parents are. The nurse gets up from her seat, smoothes down her uniform and walks calmly over to the girl. She sighs. Nigel thinks it's as if the nurse has seen the girl before, knows what is to come.

Nigel can hear muffled conversation. The girl points out the door nervously. The nurse pats her on the head. She walks around her desk and picks up the phone. Nigel watches the girl as the nurse talks animatedly into the phone. He watches the girl standing there, in front of the desk, her hands tenderly hugging her ribs, her sweater wet and torn, her hair matted and drying around her head. The girl is looking at the ground. Every so often she stares at the Emergency doors and then back to the floor. He wonders what she is doing there alone. Nigel thinks the girl is probably only ten years old.

"Jesus." Beth is lying in a stretcher. She is being wheeled out of the x-ray room. Nigel stands. "Tell them, Nigel," Beth says. "Tell them I don't need a tetanus shot. I can't believe this place."

Nigel smiles apologetically at the man who is pushing Beth. The man shrugs. "Doctor's orders."

"I just need my ankle put in a splint, wrapped up, something," Beth shouts at Nigel as the man wheels her down the hall. "Just tell him that, Nigel. Why won't anyone pay attention to what I'm saying?"

Nigel sits down again in the waiting room. He shudders. He feels a draft in the room. He changes seats.

"It figures you'd bring me somewhere like this," Beth shouts, her voice receding. "There are a bunch of idiots working here. Figures this is where you would take me."

Nigel sips his cold coffee and looks at the TV. When he glances back at the front desk both the girl and the nurse are gone. Nigel sighs.

Watching TV in the Emergency waiting room alone, on a cold, rainy night, is much better than watching TV at the cottage with Beth. This thought makes Nigel sad. He thinks of how many nights he's been sitting in Emergency rooms in the last two months. How many times he's driven furiously through the streets, Beth in pain beside him, yelling at him to hurry, hurry, hurry. And Nigel knows he should put this all together in some sort of logical pattern—Beth is unhappy, Beth is hurting herself because she is unhappy—but he has trouble thinking of it that way. He has trouble seeing beyond what he feels about her these days because she's been so hard to live with. And Nigel really wants to make a go of it, he wants to have a marriage that works. He doesn't want to be a statistic, an example of how kids of divorced parents turn out. He wants to push the odds. And he thinks he remembers every so often that he does love her, doesn't he? There must have been a reason to get married in the first place.

"Humph," Nigel says. "Humph."

"*Humph?*" The young girl from earlier is sitting directly behind Nigel.

Nigel starts.

"Did you say humph?" she asks.

Nigel smiles.

The girl smiles. She moves her chair to face Nigel.

"I didn't see you there," Nigel says. "I was just 'humphing' to myself."

"Habit?"

"Pardon?"

"Is that a habit of yours?" The young girl has a crooked grin. Her eyes are funny. Nigel can't put a finger on it but he thinks that one eye is wandering. Or maybe she is cross-eyed. Nigel doesn't want to look too closely for fear of insulting the girl.

"No," Nigel says. "Just a thing I do when I'm bored."

"I'd call that a habit." The girl's voice is high-pitched. She has a strange accent, pronounces "I" as "Ah."

"Are you all right?" Nigel sees the girl's hands are bleeding. She is holding a Kleenex to them, pressing tightly. Her knuckles are white. Her sweater, where she clutched it earlier, has handprints in blood on it.

The girl smiles mysteriously.

"There you are." The nurse comes back into the waiting room. "I've been looking all over for you."

The nurse takes the girl's hands and begins to clean them with alcohol and then bandage them. The girl screws her eyes shut but continues to smile. Nigel turns away, towards the TV, giving them privacy. He is so sad, as if the weight of the world is on his shoulders; a bad marriage, an injured or dead cat, a battered little girl. And she has been battered, or beaten, or abused somehow. It's obvious. But Nigel wants to ignore that, push it deep down, away from him. He's got too much on his plate right now. Two months of marriage and the whole world is falling apart.

There is a man on TV demonstrating spray-on hair. He holds a can up to his head and, within seconds, a dark spray covers his bald spot and he has a full head of hair.

Nigel's hair is thinning. Just in the last two months. Accidents, thinning hair, fighting. The fights. That's all they ever do anymore:

"*I didn't mean that.*"

"*Say what you mean.*"

"*Do what you say.*"

"*What do you mean?*"

What happened to making love, holding hands, looking into each other's eyes? Nigel would settle for anything about now. Even just a good tight squeeze, a tickle, some body contact. Anything.

He feels like saying *humph* again but he knows the little girl will react and he doesn't feel like explaining himself to anyone.

"God damn it," Beth shouts. She is now in a wheelchair, her leg elevated. "Just wrap it up, for God's sake, and let me go home. Nigel, tell them to wrap up my foot. If this were the city they'd have wrapped me up by now and sent me home."

Nigel looks at Beth. He tries to imagine her situation. Something has changed, she says, marriage did it, nothing is right anymore. And she's in pain now, physical pain. He gets up, walks over to her and smoothes down her hair. "Are you feeling okay?"

"Am I feeling okay? What do you mean by that? Jesus, Nigel,

you are as stupid as these people. Of course I'm in pain. My leg is killing me and no one will do anything about it. They just move it around and look at it. Get me out of this place."

Nigel looks at the man who is pushing the wheelchair. The man shrugs again. Nigel doesn't know how to take the shrug. He is embarrassed and angry, but then, as the man wheels Beth down the hall, Nigel watches her put her head in her hands and her body shakes. Nigel suddenly feels something, a tiny shiver, a little spasm, shoot through his body, but he doesn't understand it— it's been far too long since he's felt like this. The shiver dissipates quickly even though he tries to keep it there, keep feeling that shiver. Nigel wonders if maybe his life would be all right if he could do something with that feeling, if he could harness it and keep it close to his body. But he has to give up at some point and so he concentrates on the spray-on hair on TV.

Nigel can't even tell the difference between the real hair and the spray-on hair but he knows that if he saw the man close up he'd surely notice. He imagines the man caught in a rainstorm, like tonight. The spray-on hair running down his face. He smiles.

"Now don't you be laughing at that," the nurse says, happily. "My husband tried the stuff and it really works."

Nigel laughs. "Really?"

The girl begins to sing in a small whisper as the nurse finishes off the bandaging.

"It looks great. It looks like real hair."

"What about—"

"Rain?"

"Yes, rain. Or showers."

"Everyone asks about that. He just puts a little more on after the shower. He's never been stuck in the rain. I don't think it'd come off." The nurse thinks about this. "I think it's pretty sturdy stuff. It's hard to wash off. You should try it."

Nigel looks at the girl. He touches his thinning hair. He wishes it weren't thinning. He wishes it were as thick as it used to be. The girl is holding her hands out in front of her, wrapped in bandages. "What happened to you? How did you hurt your hands?" Nigel asks. He knows he shouldn't, he knows he doesn't want to find out what happened, but he suddenly can't help himself.

"We've been married twenty-five years," the nurse says.

"Really?" Nigel swallows. He looks at the young girl. He looks at her white bandages and her little mouth opens and closes as she sings and sings.

"When you've been married twenty-five years it doesn't matter if your husband's hair melts off in the rain." The nurse laughs loud and long, enjoying her joke.

The girl smiles.

The nurse purses her lips. "Never you mind what happened to her," she says to Nigel. "It doesn't matter now, does it?" The girl looks down at the floor and hums. "As long as you heal up quickly." The nurse pats her on the head. Roughly.

Nigel knew his parents were going to divorce before they even knew. He could sense it. He could feel it in the air inside the house. He also sensed that something was wrong before he was told his father had died and he felt something crazy in the air tonight as Beth slipped on the tiles in the rain.

And something is wrong with the young girl and her situation and his marriage is on the rocks and something, some bolt of lightning, something wild is going to happen soon.

"She's getting a cast on," the nurse says. "Your friend. It seems her leg is broken."

Nigel nods. He wonders why this doesn't surprise him.

"She should be ready in a few minutes."

The young girl looks at Nigel with those skewed eyes and smiles. Nigel tries to smile back. He thinks it's sad, so very sad, that the girl is in the hospital all alone late at night. Nigel drums his fingers on his seat. Childhood should be full of happiness, Nigel thinks, because adulthood is full of complication and confusion.

"Do you want a hot chocolate?" Nigel asks. "I'll buy you one."

The girl looks at the nurse who nods her head. "Yes, please," she says.

Nigel buys the girl a hot chocolate and then sits down beside her. The nurse frowns.

"What happened to your friend?" the girl asks.

"My wife? She slipped in the rain. She was running to answer the phone from the boat house to the cottage."

"Why was she running?"

"I guess she really wanted to talk to the person who was calling." Nigel stares out at the rain. The phone rang and rang and rang.

"You're not from around here, are you?"

Nigel shakes his head. "From the city."

"Did you watch *When Animals Attack*?" the girl asks.

"Yes, some of it."

"Did you see the lion in Africa?"

"No, I didn't. I saw a rhinoceros in Texas maul a man with a camera."

"Well, I was watching a lion in Africa eat a man. I was watching that and then I had to come here so I missed the ending. The lion was eating a man's arm."

Nigel doesn't know what to say. He thinks of Beth and her ankle and how it's broken and the pain she must be in and he sighs.

If he were to stay married to Beth for twenty-five years, he wonders how many days, months, years he would have to wait in hospital Emergency rooms. He wonders if this is only nerves, just getting used to marriage, but then he thinks about whether he wants to get used to this.

The girl smiles. She sips her hot chocolate. "It's good when animals attack," she says. "It's about time."

Nigel wonders what accident it will be next week. He wonders if she'll lose a finger or an arm or maybe crack her skull. Maybe she'll be in a car accident and die. Maybe she'll get eaten by a cat. Nigel chuckles. If he breaks it down like this the whole thing seems slightly ridiculous. A woman whose displeasure with her life, her husband, boils down to freak accidents, broken limbs.

"What's so funny?"

"I was imagining my wife being eaten by a cat."

The young girl laughs. "I do that," she says. "I imagine that kind of stuff all of the time."

"A little, white cat. One of those with pushed-in noses. The expensive ones." Nigel smiles. "A rhinestone collar. Nicely groomed." The girl giggles. The nurse looks at them from her desk. She turns the volume up on the TV, using the remote control in her hand.

"I ran over a cat tonight," Nigel says and when he says it he feels suddenly very sad. He puts his head in his hands and rubs his eyes.

The young girl swallows her hot chocolate loudly. She looks away. Nigel repeats what he said, "I ran over a cat tonight. In the rain."

The girl frowns. "Humph," she says.

"But it got up and ran off the road," Nigel says. "It ran away from me."

The girl brightens. "It ran away?"

"Yes."

"Then it's okay?"

"Yes, I guess. Wouldn't you think so?"

The girl smiles again. "For a minute there," she says. "I thought I was going to have to hate you too and I'm so tired of hating everyone."

Nigel looks at the young girl and suddenly feels very cold.

Beth is wheeled down the hall, she is red and flustered, her foot is in a cast. "Let's get out of here," Beth says. She seems defeated finally, worn out. "Come on, Nigel. Let's get out of here."

Nigel looks down at the floor. He tries to cheer himself up by imagining that boa constrictor wrapped around Beth's belly, but the horror of the situation hits him and he feels light-headed and weak and angry at himself. The young girl looks at Nigel as if she knows what he is thinking.

"My advice to you," the nurse whispers to Nigel as he wheels Beth out of the hospital, "is to go away. Take a holiday. Get away from the country. Spend some time in the city." The nurse laughs. "And that spray-on hair is great, really," she adds. "Give it a try."

As Nigel wheels Beth out of the hospital, he turns to wave to the young girl and the girl lifts her bandaged hands and waves back. Her stiff, little white hands seem to glow. All the way back to the cottage in the car, with Beth complaining beside him, complaining about the hospital, about the cottage, about Nigel's family, his dead father, her married life, how-sick-and-goddamn-tired-she-is-of-everything, Nigel looks carefully for any cats on the road.

Martin

Martin locks the front door and the screen door slams shut behind him. He stands on the porch for a minute, holding his rifle by his side and looking at the farms surrounding his property. He glances down to the work shed and then over to the highway, which runs north-south in front of his house. Martin's car is parked at an angle in the dirt driveway. His mailbox, at the end of the driveway, is wooden and carved in the shape of a black bear. Carved and painted. Martin carved the mailbox last year, in the winter, when he had nothing else to do. The old mailbox was rusty and worn, the door hung open and the flag was broken. The air outside Martin's house is humid and hot. The air inside Martin's house is the same.

Martin looks at his car, at his new mailbox, at the highway. He looks up at the sky. There is not a cloud in sight. He walks down the front porch, the boards creaking under his weight, and he opens the trunk of his car and he places his rifle down carefully. He climbs into his car and starts the engine. It is July. It is early Friday evening. Martin can't find a break in the traffic so it takes him ten minutes to pull out of his driveway. Once out, he speeds down the highway towards town. The cottagers are rushing past, driving to their properties before the sun falls and the moon rises.

Martin turns on the radio. It is resting beside him on the passenger seat, the wires stretched into the empty hole of the dashboard. He spins the dial until he finds something worth listening to and then settles back in his seat and adjusts his rear-view mirror. He taps his fingers on the steering wheel. The air outside rushes into the car and blows his hair, it ruffles the hair on his forearms. Martin is wearing a white T-shirt and blue jeans that are stained and faded. He is wearing running shoes covered in mud and cow manure from his late-night walks around the neighbouring properties, around the farms, through the wooded areas, down by the beach. Those late walks where the dark closes in and surrounds him, where he can be alone with the wilderness. Martin hasn't shaved in three days so there is a thick growth of stubble on his face, almost hiding his increasing jowls. He has a heavy face, a large build, small hands and bright blue eyes. Piercing eyes. His eyes are set deep in his sockets, his eyebrows large and bushy. The blue peers out of the shadow and seems to be full of light and shine.

Martin drives slowly. He watches with interest as the cottagers pull up beside him and then overtake him. He looks into their cars as they pass, at the inflatable lake toys, at the children in the back seats, at the dog with its head out the window, its tongue lolling. He looks at the parents holding maps or cans of pop, or turning to holler at their children. The mother with the scarf holding her hair down, laughing with a wide-open lipstick-red mouth. The young couple holding hands over the stick shift. The kid riding in the back seat, turned towards Martin, giving him the finger.

Darren is waiting for Martin at the crossroads, beside the old railroad track. He is sitting on a large rock and looking down the road in the direction of town, looking away from where Martin is coming to pick him up. Darren is wearing his jean jacket. Too hot for the weather, Martin thinks, but Darren has skinny arms and likes to cover them up.

"Hey there." Darren climbs into the back seat of the car. "Jesus, Martin, hook up that radio so I can sit in the front."

Martin says nothing. He turns the radio down.

Darren runs his fingers through his hair. He lights a cigarette and opens the back window. He throws the match onto the receding road. "Where are we going?"

Martin shrugs.

"Lido's?"

"Don't know."

"Let's go to Lido's."

"We could just drive."

"What good would that do?"

"What good comes out of anything," Martin says. "Give me a cigarette."

Darren hands Martin a cigarette and Martin steers with his knees as he tries to light it, the wind coming in the car and putting out the match over and over.

"Jesus, light this for me."

Darren lights the cigarette and passes it up front to Martin. The cigarette is sticky from Darren's lips.

Up ahead, near the centre of town, is the bridge over the Rodeo River. When he is crossing it Martin slows the car down. He looks at the older men leaning on the railings, their fishing lines dangling in the water.

"Could fish," Martin says.

"Shit," Darren says. "I'm dressed for a good time."

"They're always fishing."

"Every second of every day. Old men fish, Martin. Not us." Darren sniffs loudly and then balls phlegm in his throat with a deep, guttural growl. He spits out the window.

"You spit on my car," Martin says calmly, looking back over his shoulder at Darren, "and you're dead."

Darren laughs. "I'm trying to hit Mr. Randerson." He points out the window to an older man leaning into the railing looking down into the rapids. "He deserves to be hit. Don't you think?"

Martin sighs. For ten years now, on Friday nights in the summer and in the winter, he's been picking up Darren and going to Lido's for beer. He's been drinking at Lido's and doing nothing else for as long as he can remember. Martin is starting to lose his hair and Darren's hair is turning grey. There are lines on Martin's face that weren't there ten years ago, lines around his eyes and mouth. His jowls are wobbling and his stomach is fat.

"Let's do something else," Martin says. "Let's drive to Rosefield. Or Petron. Let's see if Nick is working security at the plant."

"Shit," Darren says. "I'm thirsty. Let's stop in Lido's. See who's there."

Martin pulls the car into Lido's parking lot. He sees Tommy's station wagon, Frank's new jeep and Howard's pickup. "Same old, same old."

"What's with you?" Darren says as he hops out of the car.

"Nothing." Martin stands outside his car and looks at the river. It passes across the street, meandering alongside the road the bar is on. He watches the rapids swell and fall and he looks at the beauty of it and he thinks of nothing at all. "It's just," Martin says. "I work with these guys all week. Every day."

"Yeah, so?" Darren is at the door to Lido's. "You work with Nick every day too. What's the difference? Just a couple beers and then maybe we'll do something fun."

"Nick is in the security booth. I only see him when I park my car."

"So what? Let's just get a drink. It's hot out here."

Martin follows Darren into the dark bar. The cigarette smell is overwhelming. Martin adjusts his lungs for breathing in the smoke. The air conditioning is cool and inviting.

Tommy and Howard are at the bar. They nod at Darren and Martin. Frank is at the jukebox in the corner, knocking it with balled fists.

"What's up?" Darren sits at the bar and orders two beers. Martin takes one. He drinks out of the bottle. The beer is refreshing and cold. "Goes down nice, doesn't it, Martin? Now aren't you glad you came in?"

Frank walks to the bar. "I think the damn machine is broken. It stole my quarters."

Howard laughs. "You always say that. Just drink a couple more beers and you'll think you hear music."

"Every Friday night you are amazed that the box is broken," Darren says. "Get a life."

"It wasn't broken last week."

Martin walks over to the window and looks out. The air conditioning is cooler by the window. He watches kids walking with Popsicles in their mouths along the riverbank. He can see a girl in shorts and a bikini top laughing at something her boyfriend is saying. Her breasts jiggle as she laughs, her hand is on the boy's arm and she leans into him. He sees an old man trying to fish in the rapids just up from the bar. He looks wobbly and unbalanced on the wet stones above the river. The old man pulls in his fishing line and walks away in the direction of the bridge. Martin looks at his car in the parking lot. He looks at the trunk and he thinks of his rifle lying there with the safety on.

"I wish it was snowing," Darren is saying when Martin returns to the bar. "Why doesn't it snow in the summer? Once in a while it'd be nice if it snowed."

Howard smiles. "Every second day. Hot one day, snow the next."

"The streets would be wet forever," Frank says. "We'd be walking in puddles."

"I just wish it would snow."

Martin orders another beer and then another. He drinks them

quickly. He waits for the feeling to leave his mouth. He waits for the numbness to set in.

"Remember the dog shit everywhere when it melts?" Tommy says. "I don't miss that dog shit."

"And the smell of it." Frank laughs.

"Get a dog, Tommy," Howard says. "Just get a dog and stop complaining."

"I hate dogs. They stink. And they slobber. Big gobs of slobber."

"I hate people who hate dogs."

The men laugh.

Martin notices two women sitting in a booth by the wall drinking beers and smoking cigarettes. He watches them as they talk animatedly to each other. The blonde woman waves her hands in the air and her large mouth opens and closes. She looks like a fish gasping for air. Her nose is skinny and long. Or she reminds Martin of a bird. The other woman is wearing a T-shirt that reads, FLORIDA IS FOR LOVERS. She has large breasts and a small neck. Her sunglasses are perched atop her head, holding back her mousy hair. She has beady eyes and thick eyebrows and a cold sore on her lip.

Martin's tongue is going numb.

Martin thinks about how easy it is to pull the trigger. Release the safety, point, take aim, pull the trigger. Easy as one, two, three.

The women laugh loudly. They bury their eyes in their hands and they laugh and laugh.

"You hear another one is missing," Frank is saying.

"Yeah," Tommy says. "Another one."

"They just keep disappearing. And there's nothing the same about each case. One minute they are there. The next they are gone."

"Watch out, Tommy," Darren laughs, "if you don't get a dog you'll be next."

"What's a dog going to do?"

"Bite the guy's balls off."

They laugh.

"How many is that now?" Howard asks. "Six? Seven?"

"How do you know it's a man?" Tommy asks. "Maybe it's a woman."

"I think five. I think five have gone missing this summer."

Martin orders another beer. His money is running low. He'll have to stop at the bank machine in town. He needs groceries tomorrow and he wanted to see that new movie at Mullman's Theatre on Sunday. Sunday afternoons the movies are cheap and the air conditioning is turned so high Martin brings his jacket. He likes to sit in the cold theatre in the summer with his hands in the pockets of his fall jacket. He likes to blow on his fingers to warm them. And then it's Monday, another work week at the plant, the quick flow of car parts to be inspected, the coffee breaks and lunch breaks and afternoon breaks. The sign-up sheet for the bathroom. Martin's been at the same job since high school and is learning to hate it. Martin should probably drive out to the farm to visit his mother and father on Sunday night. See how they are, see if they need anything. His sister keeps them busy, but once he went over and there was no milk in the fridge, there was nothing to stir in his coffee and his mom was complaining about a sore rash on her leg that wouldn't go away and his sister wasn't awake yet, even though it was two in the afternoon.

"Those two are looking at you, Darren," Howard says.

"Are not."

"They are. The one with the big tits and the sunglasses."

"Fuck off."

"They like skinny men." Howard laughs.

Frank says, "I've got to piss."

"I'm not skinny," Darren says.

"Try the jukebox on your way back, Frank," Tommy laughs. "Put some quarters in."

"Yeah, you're big and muscly, Darren."

"Martin's awfully quiet tonight," Howard says. "Hey, Martin, cat got your tongue?"

Martin feels lazy. He feels drained. "It's too damn hot to speak," he says. "You guys are just wasting energy."

"That's what the beer is for," Darren says. "Quick energy."

Bang, Martin thinks. Like that. Just a quick release of your finger and the bullet travels through flesh. The bullet travels. Too quick for you to see. Everything happens so fast. The tearing of the flesh, the jerking back of the body, the slow seepage of blood.

"So, what's the asshole doing with them, then?" Howard asks.

Darren shrugs. "They haven't found any bodies yet. I heard that they think he's burying them somewhere. On a farm. In the woods maybe."

"Maybe in the river," Tommy says. "Maybe he's weighing them down with stones."

"Cement, like the Mafia do."

"Maybe Darren's dad is burying them at the family farm." Howard cracks up.

"Shit," Darren says. "Yeah, right. I'm not eating fish from the river anymore, thanks to you."

The women at the booth get ready to leave. The blonde picks up her cigarette pack and lighter and puts them in her purse. The mousy-haired woman touches the top of her head to see if her sunglasses are still there. Martin watches her large breasts move under her T-shirt. She looks up at him, knowing he is watching her, and she smiles. Martin's face turns red. He feels his stubbly face. When his parents moved out of their house and let Martin have it, when they moved to the farm to live with his sister and her drunk husband, Martin had to put a mirror up in the bathroom in order to see his face while he shaved. His mother doesn't believe in mirrors, thinks they are evil, that they tempt people and make them vain. Martin laughs to think of it. It's funny now, but he grew up for twenty-something years with no mirrors in the house. He'd look at himself in the store window reflections or at the bathroom at school. He remembers being shocked at the growth of pimples on his face on Monday mornings. Pimples that hadn't been there on

Friday afternoon. And the dark hair that jutted out of his chin, his nostrils.

But now that he has a mirror in the bathroom, over the rusted sink, he feels more self-conscious than ever. He feels as if he's being watched half the time. He feels he can't piss alone anymore. He turns quickly towards the mirror and his old face is always staring back at him.

"I bet it's a cult or something," Frank says, after coming back from the bathroom. "Like a devil-worshipping thing."

"You heard that on the radio," Howard says. "I heard that too."

"What the fuck is a cult doing in this boring town?"

"Maybe it's aliens," Frank says.

"Yeah," Darren laughs. "Deserted country road. Aliens land. Take six people."

"Five."

"We'll read about it in the *National Enquirer*."

"Shit," Tommy says. "What good would a dog be against aliens?"

"Let's go somewhere," Martin says. "Let's get out of this bar."

"Not when the action has just begun," Howard says. He points towards the receding figures of the two women. As they leave Lido's and the heat wave blasts into the bar, another group of women enters. Lisa, Sue-Ann and Charlene.

"Hey," Howard shouts. "Come here. Keep us company."

The women move up to the bar and stand beside the men.

"Martin here wants to go but I want to stay and talk with you," Howard says. He puts his head on Charlene's shoulder. She shrugs him off.

"Let's go, Darren," Martin says.

"Don't go," Charlene says. "We haven't seen you two since last Friday." She laughs.

The women order beers and drink them out of the bottle. Martin watches the TV set above the bar. He watches wrestling.

Lisa says, "Did you get a load of Simon at work the other day?"

Martin sighs. "Let's not talk about work."

"Fuck off, Martin. Simon was crying. Bawling like a baby," Lisa says.

"He was more afraid of the blood," Darren says. "Is that true? Who the hell is afraid of blood? Man, I'm more afraid of shit."

Everyone laughs.

"He was pale," Sue-Ann pipes up. "God, he was white as a sheet."

"He didn't even lose his hand," Frank says. "I saw Mr. Adams lose his foot in a threshing machine when I was twelve and I didn't faint."

"Hazards of farming," Howard says.

"Nick took Simon to the hospital. They sewed him up. Supposedly he screamed a lot," Lisa says.

Martin thinks of the day his father lost his thumb. He came screaming up to the house, his hand wrapped in his white T-shirt. He was hollering and his face was turning deep purple and Martin swears his eyes were popped far out. The size of golf balls. Martin was sure he could see the ligaments that held his father's eyes in his sockets. Martin's mother took his father to the hospital and Martin was sent out into the field to find the thumb. There it was near the haystack, bloodied and drained of colour. His father's thumbnail speckled white from lack of calcium, chewed back instead of cut. Rough cuticle, callused pad. The knuckle was hairy. Martin remembers that the most. Black, thick, wiry hair. Martin took his handkerchief out of his pocket and spit on it and cleaned the thumb. Cleaned off all the dried blood. He kept waiting for the thumb to move, for it to jerk or bend or something. He was just a kid.

"I heard that the guy is raping them first and then killing them. Or maybe that he's hiding them in his house," Lisa says.

"No shit."

"Who wants another beer?" Howard asks.

"I want the damn jukebox to work," Frank says. He puts his head on the bar. "Would someone please fix the jukebox?"

"No way," Sue-Ann says. "Why would some freak be raping old men too? Weren't there two old men?"

"Yeah, and one girl. And one older woman."

"Who was the fifth?"

"I'd like a fifth of whiskey," Darren says. "Isn't that what they say in the movies?"

After he cleaned the thumb Martin wrapped it in his handkerchief and buried it. He knew that if he took the thumb to the hospital, if he rode his bike quickly through the fields, then there was a chance his father could have it sewn back on. But Martin buried the thumb instead. He buried it under the rusty mailbox he replaced just this winter.

"The fifth was a little boy, I think," Charlene whispers.

"Let's get out of here," Martin says. "Let's go down to the beach at least."

"No way," Darren says. "Too many cottagers. Too many people. No beer."

"That's always the problem, isn't it?" Howard says. "No beer on the beach."

"Big, fucking problem," Tommy says.

"No," Frank says. "The jukebox. That's the big fucking problem."

Martin goes to the washroom. He enters a stall and pisses sitting down on the seat. He bends his penis into the toilet. He sighs when the stream is strong and steady. Martin washes his hands in the sink and dries them on a paper towel. Out of habit, he glances in the mirror at his face and he rubs his eyes hard. His blue eyes look back at him.

Every day, on his way home from school, Martin would pass that old mailbox. He would stop for a minute, look down at the ground, and he would think of nothing in particular. And then he would think of that thumb down there, under the earth, and he would let that thought stay with him as he continued to walk down the driveway towards home.

Back from the bathroom, Martin orders another beer and his tongue is finally completely numb. He tastes nothing. His mind buzzes a bit. He burps quietly, holding his hand up to cover his mouth.

"I heard Franko's is closing down," Darren is saying. "I heard he's going out of business."

"Everyone is going out of business here," Howard says.

"I heard that Franko is moving to the city because he wants his daughters to go to better schools."

"And we have to lose a bakery just because of that?"

Charlene laughs. She is sitting on a barstool and her short skirt is riding high. "Is that all you care about, Tommy, doughnuts?" Her voice is quiet and controlled.

"What else is there? What else is there in the world?"

Martin pays his tab.

"Hey, Martin, where you going?"

"For a drive."

"He's in a bad mood tonight," Darren says. "Got up on the wrong side of the bed."

"Be careful out there," Lisa shouts into the noisy bar. "Be careful. There's a murderer out there."

"Hush up," says the bartender. "You'll scare the customers."

"Come back and get me later," Darren says. "I'll need a ride home."

Martin nods. He leaves the bar. The heat outside strikes him, makes him feel dizzy. He stands for a minute on the stairs, looking across the street at the river, and then he walks over to his car and gets in. He rolls down his window, starts the engine and turns on the radio. There is a news report on the disappearing people. Martin thinks he'll drive through town, back and forth, drive the main streets, until he decides what to do. He'll go to the bank machine and he'll drive past Mullman's and see what time the movie starts on Sunday.

Maybe he'll drive past the car plant and see if Nick is working the late shift in the security booth. Martin will keep him company, kill time with Nick. He likes to talk with Nick. Nice enough guy. Quiet, a little shifty. But he has a wife and kids, a real family, and he likes to show Martin pictures of his kids. Martin especially likes the photo Nick carries of his wife, pregnant with their second child, holding the first one high in the air, a smile on her face like nothing Martin has seen before. She has golden hair that glows in the sun and the baby is squealing, or laughing, mouth open wide. Martin likes that picture. He likes Nick. He likes what Nick stands for, he likes what the man's accomplished in his life. Nick doesn't hang out at Lido's every Friday night. In fact, Martin remembers that Nick sometimes drives into the city with his wife and takes in a play. Sometimes Nick goes to the community theatre in town and watches a show.

Once Nick invited Martin over for dinner. Invited him over to meet the wife and kids. Martin made the excuse that he had something else to do. He doesn't know why he did it, why he didn't go over and taste their food. And Nick was a little testy with him after that. For awhile he would only nod and wave Martin into the parking lot. He wouldn't put his head out the window of the booth to say hello.

But things are better now. Nick is back to his old self.

Martin turns the radio loud and heads the car in the direction of the plant. The rifle rattles in the trunk, bangs and rolls a bit. Martin thinks that he really should have tied it down. It could be dangerous, rolling like that, shifting around as he turns corners. Or maybe he should stop the car and take the rifle out. Put it on the back seat, or on the front seat, beside him.

Martin taps on his steering wheel to the music from the radio. He taps and he thinks he'll pull over just ahead, up there, right before the car plant. Martin can see the lights of the plant glowing over the corn fields. He can see the light from Nick's booth, a solitary shine, a warm, gentle radiance. He'll pull over and get the rifle out of the trunk. He'll put it beside him on the seat. Right beside him. Where it will stay in one place and not roll around.

Martin drives off the road and slows down on the pebbly shoulder. He stops the car. He knows that somewhere in the darkness, in the heat of the summer, there are people disappearing, falling off the face of the earth. It will be good to have his rifle beside him on the front seat. He knows there is a murderer out there, just waiting to strike again.

Hunting for Something

Tom Hunt has just opened a religious supply store on Main Street in the city. The sign out front says:

HUNTING FOR SOMETHING?
RELIGIOUS PARAPHERNALIA AND SUPPLIES

Tom took the money he received from his mother's will and quit his job at Mack's Factory where he had worked for twenty years as a machine welder. Tom misses working with fire, the quick scent of fuel, the hot-blue of the flame, but sitting behind the counter at Hunting for Something, he's come to fully appreciate running his own business. He opened the store last week, on Wednesday, and it's now Friday and he's doing a booming business. He can come in at any time, he can leave at any time, he can take a walk at lunch up and down Main and wave to the other store owners, he can watch the TV he installed behind the counter, he can be his own man. At Mack's Factory he was told when to stand up and sit down. He was told when to sneeze. Tom Hunt is completely satisfied with his new calling.

Tom was a little concerned that the word would get out that he isn't Christian, that he comes from no denomination, that his mother, rest her soul, never thought to baptize him or take him to church. He wondered for awhile if that would hurt business, if his customers, mostly nuns and priests, would stop coming if they thought the store was run by an atheist. But Tom isn't atheist, really, he's more secular. He likes to think of himself that way—a man of the world. He's open to all religions and, at the same time, no religions. Tom accepts people just the way they are, be they pure or evil, be they sprinkled with a bit of zealousness—it's all the same to him. He has no responsibility to anyone, and doesn't care to, and so whatever people believe in doesn't bother him at all. If anything, Tom thinks, his openness can only help business, make his more of an open shop.

Besides, he's been open for over a week and, so far, no one has complained. One nun did tell him the TV was on too loud, that Oprah was guffawing much too heartily, that the store should be quiet and blessed, but Tom merely understood that as her kind of zealous jealousy for Tom's being able to live life normally.

It is Friday afternoon, after lunch, and Tom is sitting high on his stool behind the counter, letting the Thai food he ate rest heavily in his stomach. The garlic and pepper scent on his breath irritates him. He has brushed his teeth in the little bathroom in the back of the store three times but still the smell lingers, the taste lingers. Tom sits on his stool and blows into his cupped hands and smells his breath.

He watches an ad on TV for car polish and then one for diapers. A fat baby, naked but for a tight diaper, holds his hands up to a shiny cartoon star floating high above and tries to catch it. Tom supposes that catching the star may symbolize the leak-proof quality of the diapers, but he isn't sure. He's never had kids, nor a wife, and he's never wanted anything of the sort. His life has remained uncomplicated and controlled. Nothing to take away from him, nothing to give. Tom mutes the commercial and waits for the talk show to continue.

The bell above the door rings and a man wearing blue jeans and a black leather jacket steps into the store. The man looks around and picks up a few items as if noting the prices. He moves around the store. Tom begins to feel slightly nervous because he isn't yet used to approaching people, making a sale. He would rather sit on his stool and look at the floor, give people their buying privacy. But all of the store owners on Main Street have told him it is better to talk to your customers, look them in the eye, make contact. They have told him that their businesses thrive on the personal well-being of their customers.

So Tom says, "Hello. Can I help you?"

The man looks up, startled. He looks quickly at Tom. "I didn't see you there," he says.

Tom smiles. "Well, I was. I am."

"Yes," the man says. "Yes, you are."

"Can I help you with anything? Are you looking for something in particular?" Tom wants to say, *are you hunting for something* but he thinks he might giggle if he uses the store's name in a sentence. It took him weeks to come up with that name and now it seems so obvious—religious supplies—Tom Hunt—Hunting for Something? Tom shakes his head.

The man shrugs. He runs his hand over a statue of Jesus on the cross and then lets his palm rest on a Bethlehem snow globe, cupping it. Tom wishes the man would shake the globe and see the sprinkles, see the snow, like diamonds, fall down upon the desert city. He knows the man would buy it if he just shook it. Tom marvels continuously at that globe. He has seven stored upstairs by the foot of his bed. Seven he just didn't want to sell. And he shakes them each before he turns out the light each night. Shakes them up and watches the desert get cold.

"I was looking for something," the man starts. But then he stops talking and glances down at his boots. Tom looks at them. They are black leather cowboy boots. The design on the boots matches the one on the back of the man's leather jacket: a cross-stitched eagle. Tom has been running this business for only a little over a week but he was getting used to the nuns and priests, the black outfits and clerical collars—he certainly didn't expect to see a man dressed like this walk into his store.

"You were looking for something?" Tom says, hoping to jog the man's memory.

"Yes," he says. "Something."

"Can I help you find it or would you rather just wander? You can just look, you know. You don't have to buy." Tom shakes his head. He can't get used to selling. Personally he would rather be left alone when he walks into a store. He would rather be completely ignored. But it's bad for business, he knows, to tell people not to buy, to discourage people from purchasing his products and tell them to wander around touching things, leaving fingerprints on everything.

The man smiles nicely but says nothing, and continues walking up and down the aisles of the store.

Tom turns back to the TV. A talk show about aging and baby boomers. Something about how the cosmetics industry is making a killing selling carcinogenic makeup to help women stay young. Tom tsks. He is constantly reassured as to why he stayed single, unmarried, unhitched. He need only look around at the other half of the world, look closely at their fears and concerns.

Tom looks at his store. He looks at how tidy everything is, arranged by size, by price, by category. Everything is finely dusted and washed, the windows gleam, the carpet is vacuumed. He is proud of all his hard work. Of the hours he spent painting the store, making it right. He is pleased with the way he priced the products—stickers on the base of most things so that the price doesn't leap out at you, so that you have a chance to appreciate the beauty of the object before you know how much it costs. Tom likes that.

He thinks that customers will then have a harder time refusing to buy the item.

"Oh my," Tom heard one nun say to another yesterday. "Look at that pose." They were staring hard at a small miniature of the Last Supper. "Just look at the beautiful eyes." The nun bought the miniature, even after she turned it over and gasped at the amount. "Oh dear," she said. "But it's worth it, isn't it?" And Tom wrapped it in crepe paper and packed it in a gift box. He made sure the nun thought what she bought was precious, that what she had spent her hard-earned money on (and Tom doesn't know if nuns earn money the same way other people do) was worth buying, was something she'll cherish.

Tom thinks, what's the cost of a little gift box in the grand scheme of things? What's the cost involved in making a customer want to come back to the store? It hurts no one and takes barely anything out of Tom's pocket. As a matter of fact, if he gift-wrapped everything for everyone he could up the price, cover his costs, so to speak, and make some money. Buy a bigger TV. Mount it above the security cameras where everyone who entered the store could see. Tom's been in the malls and clothing stores, the popular stores, and he knows that a little loud music and a flashing TV brings in customers. No matter what that other nun said.

Tom scratches his head. Some dry skin sprinkles on the counter. It makes him think again of the snow globe.

Tom knows his enthusiasm for his store will soon run dry. It's bound to happen. He's seen it happen up and down Main Street. In the twenty years that he's walked this street to and from Mack's Factory, he's seen at least one hundred store changes. He's seen people come and go. It's all because they burn out. That initial feeling of success and satisfaction runs dry. They start losing money, losing patience, getting robbed and then …

Getting robbed?

Tom looks at the man in the leather jacket and cowboy boots standing before him. He sits up straighter on his stool.

"Excuse me," the man says. It seems he's been trying to get Tom's attention for a few seconds. He is standing directly in front of Tom and staring intently into Tom's eyes.

"Yes?"

"Are you all right?"

"Yes." Tom feels sweaty. Too much pepper in that Thai food, he thinks.

"I was just wondering," the man begins.

But then the door opens and two nuns and a priest come laughing into the store. The bell above the door jingles as it shuts behind them. The man, interrupted in mid-sentence, stops talking and looks again at his boots. Tom wonders for a minute if the man has stepped in something outside of the store and is surreptitiously wiping it off on his nice, clean carpet. He sniffs loudly but doesn't smell anything foul.

"Can I help you find something?" Tom leans towards the man, feeling slightly annoyed. He's missed half his program and now the store is busy. The man is a nuisance. Just bored. Has nothing to do. Here to bug him, pester him. "Do you want to buy anything?"

"No, I ..." the man looks around, looks lost. The nuns and priest wander loudly around the store, touching everything in sight. One nun is wearing white gloves and she slyly rubs a finger over several surfaces as if testing for dust. "I can't find what I'm looking for. I've been looking. I just can't find it."

"But you haven't said—" Tom begins.

And then the man turns on his booted heels, quickly, and rushes out of the store.

Tom looks back down at the TV. He looks at the woman whose entire face peeled off after she wore a mud-mask for more than the allotted twenty minutes. He looks at the burned marks on her chin and cheeks, at the scabbing, uncomfortable, painful red blistery parts. It baffles his mind, this, Tom thinks. Just baffles him.

The nuns and the priest buy candles, matches and several "Congratulations on Your Conversion" cards. One of the nuns takes a pocketful of candies from the complimentary dish Tom has placed on the counter. She takes a handful and fills up her pocket. Twice. Tom gives her a friendly smile. He knows she'll be back.

The store is empty again and Tom hasn't moved from his stool. His breath still reeks and his stomach aches. He is filling up with gas. He's getting too old to eat Thai food, he thinks. He should be having soup and crackers for lunch, something easier to digest.

When Tom's mother died, it surprised Tom how much money she had saved. Having lived in her house on her pension until the day she died, Tom had also managed to save quite a bit. Now that he thinks about it, all those meals of Kraft Dinner or baked beans, he can see how cheaply they both lived. After he buried her, Tom put all their money together, sat down with a financial planner, researched store options and bought this empty building. Lock, stock and barrel. He bought everything. And then he quit his job as a welder. He converted the upstairs into storerooms and a small apartment, moved in, painted the downstairs, and then walked up and down Main Street for a month trying to determine what was lacking in stores, what the needs of the people were. He didn't immediately think of religious supplies. It wasn't obvious. He thought first of a flower shop, or a variety store, or an underwear emporium. But all those things were available in some way or another up and down Main—the variety store sold flowers, for example— and so Tom searched far and wide for the most lucrative business he could find. Something that would never go under.

And he found it. Other than funeral homes, there is no other business, in Tom's estimation, that people desire more than a religious supply store. Where else do the faithful turn to buy their prized objects? Where else do the clergy buy their clothes? Their rosaries? Their prayer books, hymn sheets, figurines, statues, candles, etc.? Tom saw a niche that was waiting to be filled. Of course there are other religious supply stores in the city, but Tom was sure his would be the cleanest, the most accessible, and, most importantly, in the best location—Main Street. Where else? The seminary is located over on Monroe and there are four churches just blocks away.

And Tom plans to branch out, fill the needs of the other religions and cultures in his society—Hinduism, Buddhism, maybe even some Jewish or Muslim supplies.

Tom gets off his stool and stretches. The talk show on aging is over and there are more babies in diapers chasing cartoon stars. And then he sees the man with the leather jacket again. He is standing across the road peering over at Tom's store, smoking a cigarette. No, a cigar. Tom is sure it is a cigar the man is smoking. The man puffs once, twice, looks at his cigar and then looks at Tom's store and then down at his boots.

Can it be possible that the man is staking out his store? Planning to rob him? Or perhaps he is looking to injure Tom, just for fun. Tom has heard of gangs of men who terrorize store owners, beat them up, and then collect protection money. Protection from themselves, Tom supposes. Tom saw a show once, *Oprah*, or *Jerry Springer*, or maybe it was *Cops*, about a gang of young boys who terrorized a variety store owner until she shot them all one day when they came in to buy milk for their breakfast cereal. Tom doesn't want to get that paranoid. Besides, the man is alone and looks harmless enough. He is clean-cut and his boots and jacket aren't anything out of the ordinary for the city or for Main Street. Tom has seen some priests who have looked more threatening than the man across the street. The man continues to puff and Tom continues to look out of the store and wonder.

The day ticks on. Tom is disturbed in his reveries several times. He watches two more talk shows and a soap opera he's been following all week. But each time a customer leaves Tom looks out again at the street and at the man leaning on a light pole. The man doesn't move. He just stares. And he smokes cigar after cigar after cigar. Tom is sure the man will get sick if he continues to smoke so many cigars. He is sure of this because once, when he was a bit younger, Tom smoked six cigars in a row and ended up vomiting on the card table during a poker game with some people from work. That was the first time he had been asked out and he was never asked back. Tom has always been a bit of a loner, a quiet man, and this suits him fine. He doesn't need friends to have a good time. Tom knows if he wanted to he could make plenty of friends, but it's in his nature to be alone. He likes being alone. He likes the feeling of space he gets from being solitary in his mind. When too many people are talking at once Tom feels as if his head is going to explode. And the strain of keeping up an interesting conversation, of holding his own side, is more than he can bear. That's what he likes about TV. Someone else carries the conversation and there are no uncomfortable gaps. No silences. No white space or nervous fidgeting times. Tom can sit back, his arms crossed in front of him, and look down at the TV behind the counter, at the world in the box.

Out of the blue, it is 5 p.m. and time to close up the store. Tom is always surprised at how quickly the day goes now. When he was a machine welder he would be checking his watch every hour or so, having to listen to Fred or Bob go on and on and on about their exploits, their families, their boats or cars, but now, owning this store, he has time to watch TV, to let his mind wander, and when it wanders he loses track of time. It's a wonderful feeling, time passing quickly, the sun on the front of the store gone now and the inside lit up by a warm glow in the early spring sky.

Tom moves towards the front door to turn the OPEN sign to CLOSED. He locks the door and pulls the blind down. He turns off the TV. He turns the lights on in the display windows (to lure potential customers at night) and he turns the lights in the rest of the store off. Emptying out his cash register in the dark, Tom catches movement at the front window. He sees a glint of something metal, something reflected in the waning sunlight. But then, when he looks up, there is nothing there. Tom looks across the street for the man in the leather jacket but he is gone. Tom shivers. The store is silent without the TV on and Tom's breath seems loud and guttural, almost unnatural.

He thought working with fire was dangerous, but the thought of being stalked, intruded upon, robbed, watched, is filling him with dread.

Weigh the pros and the cons, Tom thinks. And the cons are imaginary—the pros are real. He hasn't yet been robbed, but he enjoys his store, he loves this kind of life. This solitariness. This emptiness. And look how much money he can sock away in the bank tonight. Tom counts the money and places it in his bank bag. He zips up the bag, rolls it and puts it under his belt buckle and shirt. Then he takes his coat off the peg at the back of the store, puts it on, zips it up, and leaves the store, startled for a second by the jingling bell above him.

Tom walks to the bank quickly. It unnerves him to carry this much money on his body. It makes him feel exposed, naked, vulnerable. He has never felt as if he were worth anything to anyone but his mother, but carrying a couple hundred dollars like this every evening, to place in his bank account, always makes him feel like he is worth a million bucks.

Tom waves politely up and down the street at the other store owners who wave back as they close up shop. He feels like a king. Or at least royalty. Tom feels as if he belongs to an upper echelon of people—store owners, businessmen and women. Awnings are rolled in, sidewalks are swept, displays in the windows are taken down or locked up. Everyone is going home for supper. Tom makes it to the bank, deposits the bag and walks back down Main Street towards the store, intending to head up to his apartment, price some more figurines, have a late supper and watch TV in bed. The thought of his seven snow globes glistening with the light from the lamppost outside his window makes him feel sleepy. But, as he nears the store he is suddenly awake. There Tom sees the man in the leather jacket standing in front of the door, looking in. Tom stops. He watches the man. The man places his hand on the doorknob and turns it. Then the man shakes the locked door hard, kicks it a bit, and rests his forehead on the cold glass.

Tom doesn't know whether to approach the man or turn away. He thinks he might be safer if he went to the Pizza Factory, had a nice dinner, and came home later, but then he wonders if, left alone, the man will do damage to his store. Or perhaps he will hide and, when Tom strolls back along Main Street, the man will jump out at him. And, on a pizza-full stomach and a couple of mugs of beer, Tom might not be able to protect himself.

Why pick my store, Tom thinks? Why mine? Unless the man knows how lucrative this business is, unless the man has robbed this kind of store before ...

But all his money is locked safe in the bank. Tom doesn't even leave five dollars in the float. The tray is open so that anyone peering in can see that it is empty. His store is locked up for the night. And Tom is free to walk away. Let the police deal with a man banging his head on a window. Tom can go eat pizza and relax.

Tom turns.

But for some reason Tom turns back. He walks up to his store, up to the man, and says, "Can I help you with anything?" It's as if by owning a store, a religious store, Tom can be confessor and forgiver. As if he's invincible. Tom suddenly feels the weight of the woman with the burned and peeled face on TV this afternoon crash down upon him. He feels her sorrow, her guilt, her sadness, her fear. Tom wishes he could reach out and stroke the woman's cheek, tell her that faith will make everything better, but then Tom smiles at his idea because it's the idea of a salesman, a store owner. If she is faithful, he will sell more religious supplies. Faith. What is it really?

Swivelling on his booted heels, the man in the leather jacket doesn't have time to disguise the pained expression in his eyes. Tom is stunned by the look. The man quickly glances down at his boots.

"What's wrong? Can I help you?" Tom tries again. His shoulders and neck and arms are tense. He hasn't felt this nervous since he was a small boy and the other boys at school would turn away from him on the playground. Or turn towards him and taunt him and kick him and beat him.

"I'm looking for something—"

"Yes?" Tom was once looking for something, looking to be saved, but he found it here in his store. Complete isolation, complete control. A store owner. He can sit high on his stool and look down at the world. He can sell or refuse sale. He can talk to the priests, to the nuns, or talk to no one at all. He is saved, he supposes. He is safe.

The man stands with his arms dangling by his side. "You closed the store. I'm looking for something—"

"It was five o'clock," Tom says. "I close the store at five o'clock. I'm open again at nine tomorrow."

"But you were busy all day," the man says. "I couldn't come in when you were so busy."

Tom raises his eyebrows. He knows there were moments in his day when the store was completely empty, moments when the man could have walked across the street and entered the store and bought whatever it is he was looking for.

"What do you need?" Tom asks.

"I need," the man says. "What you have."

"What?"

"I need what you have."

"I don't understand."

The man shrugs. "Neither do I."

Tom looks closely at him. "Are you all right?" Tom asks. "Can I take you to the doctor?"

The man laughs suddenly. His mouth open, his laugh echoing around the now-empty Main Street.

"The doctor," the man says. "That's funny."

"Look," Tom says. "I have to go home now. I have to go up to my apartment and eat supper and watch TV. You can come back tomorrow if you need something from the store."

The man stops laughing and looks up at Tom's blackened apartment window. "You live up there?"

"That's not important," Tom says.

"Okay," the man says. He stands back from Tom and looks at him. "Okay, here's the story. I've done something bad. Very bad. And I'm looking for something—" the man pauses and looks over his shoulder, "—something that will take it all away. Something that will make everything better."

Tom stands completely still.

"Something," the man now whispers. "I'm looking for something. Can you help me?"

All Tom wanted was to open a little store, have a nice income, settle into his advancing, lonely, quiet age like a mother hen. He wanted to roost. No more talking, always talking, to the other welders at work. About their wives, their kids, their vacations, their ups and downs. No more taking care of his elderly mother. Fetching her soda crackers and licorice sticks. Nothing. No one. Tom wanted to sit on his stool behind his counter loaded with rosaries and votive candles, silver crosses and Jesus figurines, and think about nothing, absolutely nothing. He assumed the religious who entered his life, walked in and out of his store, would be quiet and contained, would have no problems that needed discussing. Nothing more important than a rip or a stain in a clerical collar, a broken crown of thorns. And now, in one day, a week into the job, this man in front of him has made him again be beholden to someone, again have to take responsibility for another man's actions.

Tom sighs.

The man before him sighs, mimicking Tom. "Something," he whispers. "I'm hunting for something, I guess, something to make everything better." He laughs politely.

Tom looks into the man's eyes. He searches that painful expression, those sad and lonely pupils, and he says, "Come in then. We'll find whatever it is you are looking for."

"Thank you," the man says. "Thank you."

Tom thinks suddenly that life is about balance. About the balancing, tilting, careful weighing of what is important and what is not.

After opening the door of the store, listening intently for the jingle of bells above and turning on the lights, Tom leads the man in, places a hand on his shoulder and walks him forward into the cleanliness, over the fresh-vacuumed carpet. He feels a bit like God. Or Jesus. Leading the injured forward. The sick. The needy. "I found what I was looking for, I guess," Tom says. "I guess I really did. Didn't I?" Tom smiles. "Maybe you can find what you are looking for too."

The man walks slowly up and down the aisles of Hunting for Something, his hands in his leather jacket pockets, staring intently down at all the items before him. And Tom watches the man move. He sits up high on his stool, the TV flickering below him, and he watches the man wander slowly up and down his store. The black sky outside is awash with stars. It startles Tom that he can see so many stars shining high above Main Street in the city. Like a Bethlehem snow globe, all glittery and alive. And then a feeling of somethingness creeps into Tom's soul. A somethingness which quickly replaces the nothingness that was there before. Maybe, Tom thinks, maybe this is the way of the world.

Convenience

I've been waiting at the front counter for ten minutes. Julie is in the back, fidding with something big. Tidying up. A box. I can hear her groaning, pulling it around. I can hear the box slide across the floor. Ten minutes. She's swearing but says she doesn't need my help. She's okay, she says from the back. She can do it on her own.

"What are you doing tonight?" Sam asks. He stands behind the counter picking his face. Erupted pimples everywhere. He looks at his fingers after he's picked. He wipes them on his cords. I look away.

"Going out."

"Out where?"

"I'll be there in a minute, Steve," Julie calls from the back. "I just have to clean up."

"Somewhere," I say. I don't know where we are going, and, even if I did, I wouldn't tell Sam. He'd probably come with us.

Lock up the store and climb into the back seat of my car and pick his face wherever we were going. Get his goo everywhere. Stare at Julie. He's that kind of person.

A group of teenagers comes into the store and heads straight for the bank machine. In the ten minutes I've been here waiting for Julie, that's all people have come into the store for. The bank machine. They take money out and then they don't spend it in the store. They take the money away and spend it somewhere else. Maybe at the pizza place next door. Sam stands there, picking. Occasionally he sells a package of cigarettes. Nothing else.

The teenagers are loud at the bank machine. One boy picks up a *Penthouse* on the rack beside him and starts making loud slurping noises at the naked women inside.

"So, where is somewhere?" Sam asks.

"What?"

"Where do you think you're going?" Sam sits down on the stool behind the counter. Settling in.

"I don't know."

"You've got to go somewhere." Sam picks at an especially large pimple and it begins to bleed. I look back at the teenagers. The boy with the *Penthouse* has rolled the magazine up and has put it in his sleeve. I see him do this. Sam sees him do this. I look at Sam.

"Hey," Sam shouts. "Put that back." Sam's voice cracks. His face turns pink. The pimples stand out against the colour.

The boy laughs at him, gives him the finger, and walks out the store with the magazine in his sleeve and his group of friends behind him. They are all laughing. Hard.

Sam looks at his shoes. Picks nervously.

"What can you do?" he says. He giggles. His face is almost purple.

I look up and Julie is standing in the back corner, by the staff door. She is looking at me, then she is looking at Sam, then looking at both of us. She sighs.

"You look great," I say.

"Yeah," Sam echoes me. "You do. You always do."

"Thanks." But Julie doesn't mean it.

Julie comes towards me and takes my hand and pulls me out of the store with her and into the dark night.

"Bye, Sam," I say.

"Bye, Steve. Bye, Julie."

Julie says nothing.

Is she angry at Sam? At me?

"Why didn't you do something?" she says as she settles herself into my car.

I start the engine to warm us up. I look over at her. She has her jaw in that position, that way of tightening it, that way of holding it stiffly, the creases around her lips that show the anger on her face.

"Do what?"

"You could have helped Sam stop those kids. They are always coming in and stealing magazines."

"What was I supposed to do? It's not my job." I drive down the street, not knowing where we are going. It's late and I'm tired. I was up early this morning playing basketball at the YMCA before work. "Besides," I say, "they could have had a knife or a gun or something."

Julie laughs. "Ha," she says. "A gun."

"How do you know?"

"How do you know anything?" Julie says. She scowls at the road.

Off to a good start. We're driving forward but not really going anywhere.

"Where are we going?" Julie sighs.

"I don't know. Where do you want to go?"

Julie shrugs. I drive on aimlessly. We sit in silence for awhile. At the stoplights I reach over and fiddle with the radio but there is nothing good coming out of it. I think of Sam back there at the store. Alone. Picking his face and sitting on the stool.

"Last week," Julie says, quietly, "Sam had to go to the doctor. It was just me at the store. Last week." She pauses here. Waits. Looks out her window. She is silent. I keep driving. I drive through town, up one side and down the other. I don't stop. Then she starts again, as if she had never stopped talking. "I'm never alone at the store, you know. I'm always with Sam there. I didn't feel safe. I was nervous. Not like Sam would stop anything. Shit, kids steal all the time and he just lets them walk out the door. But just having him there is, I don't know, safer. In a weird way." Again, she pauses. As if we have all night for this story. As if I'm not tired. "So, anyway, this girl comes in with her baby in a stroller. She must have been only sixteen. Younger than me, for sure. The baby was about a year old. Way too young to have kids. Can you imagine? Can you imagine that, Steve? Having kids. At my age?"

I nod. If I say anything now it'll ruin Julie's train of thought. Besides, her jaw has softened and I think we still might have a nice night. Maybe end up together here, in my car, steaming it up.

"The girl hands me some sort of pamphlet. She says something to me but I can't really hear her as she's all bundled up in her winter coat. She hands me the pamphlet purposefully, though, like she knows me and is giving me this specially. Then she takes a chocolate bar off the rack, hands it to her little baby, and leaves the store. Turns the stroller around and walks out. It was really quick. Only a matter of seconds." Julie is smiling at the memory. I can see the baby holding the chocolate bar, the bundled-up girl. I can see Julie, astonished, at the counter, all alone. Sam not there. The store quiet and warm.

"Wait, but she didn't pay?" I ask.

"She just walked out without paying. I didn't think babies could eat chocolate."

"And you just got mad at Sam for—"

"Steve, that's not the point. Listen to this. This is a good story."

"Okay." I've pulled the car up in the park. We watch the empty swings, the slides, the wind on the lake. Julie slides closer to me, puts her hand on my leg. I feel the warmth of it through my jeans.

It makes me think of last week, in her parents' basement and how close we always get. It makes me think that I have to get a girlfriend who doesn't live at home. I have to get a girlfriend who isn't in grade twelve. I've been out of school, working, for two years now. And I'm dating a high school girl. But then I look at her and think, God she's great-looking. And she's nice. And interesting. She tells these interesting stories all the time. They always have a point to them. So I feel her hand on my leg and how warm it is and I think all these things and suddenly it hits me that I might just love Julie. I might even want to marry her someday. That's the kind of feeling it is. Sticky. It hits me in the chest. I can feel my heart beating under her hand, in my thigh. I can see her lips, her long eyelashes, her dark eyes in the overhead light from the park. The car is off and starting to cool down. Julie sighs. That's another thing. High school girls still sigh. The girls I work with don't sigh. Ever. They get into the working world and it's as if they lose all the melodrama that followed them through school. All the shrieks and shouts and giggles and sighs. All the stuff that made them fun and wild. The stuff I hated when I was in high school. But now they are sullen and angry. Now they don't like their jobs, have rent to pay, car loans, need to find a boyfriend immediately in order to get them out of this shit job and into the world of babies and marriages and houses and mortgages. Or something like that. That's all they seem to talk about—other girls' marriages. I'm trying to sell insurance and they are talking about winter weddings and who is wearing white or ivory or whatever.

"The point is," Julie says. "The pamphlet. That's the point."

"What was it for?" I'm thinking about Sam and his pimply face, his picking and scabs. I'm thinking about how he smells, like medicine, and how he's always worked at that store. Forever, it seems. He looks at Julie in that way that bugs me. That way that pimply teenagers look at each other when they are in love. Like a dog. Like a puppy. I used to go into that store to get smokes and magazines and chocolate bars when I was in high school and Sam would be there. And he hasn't changed much in years. He must be only eighteen or nineteen years old now, but he looks about twelve. The only thing different is the braces. They came off sometime when I wasn't paying attention. Maybe Sam could date one of the girls at my work? Maybe he could get married. Have kids.

"Are you listening to me?" Julie looks at me now, takes her eyes off the swings Takes her hand off my thigh. There is a cold patch there now. My heartbeat stops.

"Yes. I'm listening."

"She had a baby, Steve. She was just a young kid with a baby."

"And a stolen chocolate bar." I laugh.

"Yeah, that too." Sigh. She looks at me. Hard.

"What kind of pamphlet did she give you?" And suddenly, looking at her looking at me, it occurs to me that I don't want to know what kind of pamphlet it is. I don't want to know because it would make the story end. It would give the story Julie is telling some sort of purpose, some sort of moral reason for being. Julie's like that with her stories. There is always a reason for telling them. And the reason often applies to me. Like when she told that story last week about the hippo and the turtle somewhere who have become family. The hippo treats the turtle like his mom or something. The point of that story was that all different people should be able to get along. She told me this story just after I complained about my boss. He's a racist idiot. He's having an affair on his wife. His wife who does everything because he's a man and so therefore doesn't need to lift a finger around the house or with the kids. He's a jerk but Julie thinks that everyone out there, in the world, has a soft spot like a baby's head. If you just look hard enough. The turtle looked hard at that baby hippo and found that soft spot, that one thing that made all the difference.

I can't imagine finding a soft spot on my boss.

"It was a religious pamphlet," Julie says, shaking me out of my thoughts. "Those kind that are in churches stuffed in with the Bibles."

"Oh," I say. Of course, I think. A religious moral. Not that Julie is religious but that's the kind of point she likes to make with her stories. Ever since she read that Flannery O'Connor woman in grade eleven she's been trying to pull in some sort of religious feeling to her stories. Be good to others. Look for the soft spot. Hippos and turtles.

Sam. It must have been because I didn't help Sam in the store when those kids stole the magazine. That's what started this story. So the pamphlet must have said something about helping others in their times of need. I nod.

Sam really needs to get a girlfriend. Or a job. Especially, though, a girlfriend. He's got to stop drooling over Julie. He's got to give up.

Julie says *abortion* so quickly that I am startled and look straight at her.

There are tears in her eyes.

"I'm only seventeen years old," Julie says.

I'm confused. She's looking at me again with those dark eyes. Tears in them. Why tears?

But we haven't. But there hasn't been a time. A moment. There has been nothing. Abortion, I think.

"The girl was handing out pamphlets about abortion and the religious horror of it all," Julie says. She is crying now. "Can you believe it? There were pictures of the babies. Pictures of fetuses." Crying hard, she sniffs loudly.

"We haven't..." I begin. "Why are you crying?"

"Shut up, Steve. Just shut up." Julie turns to the side window. Turns her shoulders awkwardly away from me.

Abortion? I want to turn her towards me, pull her close, explain to her that we haven't done anything yet. There's no way she could be pregnant. Doesn't she know what sex is? Doesn't she know anything? High school girls, I say to myself. What are they teaching them? I try to sigh internally. I don't want to move an inch in any way in case Julie panics. I want to stay completely still.

"I wasn't getting my wisdom teeth out last month," Julie whispers.

"Julie," I laugh. I can't help it. "We haven't."

Too much religion. Too much Virgin Mary. Baby Jesus. Flannery O'Connor.

"Don't you know anything? Can't you figure anything out?"

She turns to me then, her face full of venom. I can see in her face the look she will have when she is old. I can see who she would be in the offices next to mine in the insurance company. I can see the jaw, the anger, the wisdom of that hard face.

And Julie then hisses one word at me. Just that one little word that changes everything. It changes pamphlets and young girls with babies and kids who steal *Penthouse*s and high school and convenience stores, which really, if you think about it, aren't all that convenient. My perception of the world sways a bit. Changes. The blink of an eye and suddenly I don't know what to think anymore.

Julie says, "Sam," and I start the car up immediately, back out of the park, and drive her home.

Every Summer, in Every Watery Town all over the World, There Is at Least One Drowning

As it was, she was bored silly of working at the A&P. But that was only the beginning of her troubles. There was her mother, always her mother. Freddie Tourniquet, Jr. too. And there was Leroy, the delinquent stock boy in the cooler section. And Sarah-Jean, the bagger two checkout points down from her own tight position at checkout seven. Sarah-Jean rushing as if it were the bagging Olympics. Trying to get in with the boss, advance to checker status. As if it were all about how fast you went.

Marianne knows it's about much more than speed. The vegetables, for example. And the eggs. It's about the way the fruit rides in your bag, whether or not a customer asks for paper or plastic, it's about the way to bend a banana around a loaf of bread without denting or bruising.

Telltale marks of a bad checker.

Speed, though. This summer Sarah-Jean and Leroy have noticed something seductive about speed that Marianne fails to pay attention to. At least that's how they put it in the parking lot after work. Seventeen years old, their last irresponsible summer, really, and Marianne still knows nothing about stomach-dropping speed, about the beauty of going so fast you disappear.

"It's not your car, Leroy," Sarah-Jean says. "It's the speed of the contraption."

"It's the colour," Leroy says. "She said she'd prefer orange to red."

"Colour," Sarah-Jean says, "is just an excuse. It has nothing to do with anything."

Sarah-Jean's face is doughy. Pretty, though. Marianne thinks that the doughiness of her face is an unfortunate thing as it hides the brightness of her eyes. It hides the way her smile lines would crease if they had space and breathing room.

Space, Marianne thinks. It's more about space than speed.

And now it's a Thursday afternoon, the hottest part of the day. The sun is streaming in the windows at the A&P and Charlie Folks is rushing around pulling down the heavy screens as the people in line-ups one through eight shift and perspire heavily. Marianne is on her ninth bag for some woman juggling two screaming children. Sarah-Jean, down at five, has just finished up with her customer and is smiling sweetly at Leroy in the freezer section.

"Do you want bubble gum?" the juggling woman asks her children. "Candy bars? What is it you want?"

Marianne notes that Leroy's head is the size of a large cauliflower and his ears stick out like large tongues from the side of his head. Leroy puts his vegetable head in the freezer and pulls it out again. He laughs a bit and waves at Marianne. But she ignores him and so he waves to Sarah-Jean, who continues her breakneck-speed bagging but still manages to wave back.

Marianne has been with Leroy all summer. She's not proud of

it. But he took her bathing suit off at the beach one of the first days she joined him there, his hands twisted up in the bikini strings as if he were about to start knitting, and turned to her naked body with such devotion in his dumb eyes that it struck her hard.

Marianne has a soft spot for puppies and kittens. For cats with missing limbs. For dogs with mangled ears. Raccoon babies screeching over her attic bedroom in the spring.

Marianne's mother worked as a checkout girl until she married Marianne's father. Her grandmother was a summer-bagger. It's a tradition in the family. A rite of passage, a necessary evil in order to toughen you up for the rest of your life.

Marianne hates it.

Leroy puts his head in the freezer. He takes his head out. A woman reaching for ice cream glares at him.

Sarah-Jean bags her last customer and throws her hair over her shoulders and wipes the sweat from her upper lip. She's due for a lip wax, a bikini-line wax, an all-over-the-body wax. Marianne's hairlessness, her freckles and sun-stroked hair, seem to be the cause of Sarah-Jean's teenage anger this summer. Her angst. Her hormonal shifts. One look at the perfectness of Marianne can have Sarah-Jean's stomach roiling like she's on an ocean liner in a storm. And Sarah-Jean knows about rocky boats, as she's lived on a houseboat most of her life. Well, it's not really a houseboat but it's a house right beside the Sandy Cove Marina in the bad part of town, so she likes to think it's a houseboat and likes to think that she sleeps at night with the sound of the waves around her, not the drunks coming from the bars, not the crash of broken bottles and screams of women in wicked, helpless, undesirable circumstances.

Another thing is that Marianne lives on the hill overlooking the Sandy Cove Marina. That's enough to make any hot-blooded, jealous teenage girl angry.

And, although Sarah-Jean would like one of those blond football-boys from the hill, like Freddie, she'd settle for Leroy and his antics any day if it would mean grabbing something meaty away from little Miss Marianne. Besides, Sarah-Jean reminds herself, beggars can't be choosers. Leroy lives right near Sarah-Jean. In fact, his dad drinks with her dad, rolls drunkenly home with his arms around the other man. The getting should be obviously easy. But it hasn't been. All summer long she's tried, but Leroy has eyes for Marianne and Marianne likes to think she's goddamned Mother Theresa rescuing the leper. All Marianne is doing is postponing a worse ache. Sarah-Jean knows this.

So Sarah-Jean has decided that if she couldn't get Leroy easily she'd have to try the hard way—she'd have to be best friends with Marianne.

And, throughout the summer, Sarah-Jean has come to the conclusion that it's easier to lie down with a rattlesnake or tuck an octopus under the sheets than it is to befriend Marianne Borowski. Dangerous occasions like those two are easier than making her your best, best, wonderful, all-time, good girlfriend. This doesn't make Sarah-Jean stop trying. Sarah-Jean would like to think she's persistent. Anyone else would call her just plain stupid.

Charlie Folks yells at Leroy to get his damn head out of the freezer. He's letting out all the cold and the ice cream is going soft. Charlie holds up a box of ice cream and squeezes it to prove his point. Ice cream runs down his arm.

It is as if she is a missionary, Marianne thinks. Working with the savages. Coming down off her hill to get a tough skin, to better her mind for the material richness that lies ahead. Marianne's mother thought the grocery store experience was good for her. She thought it made her never forget where she came from. Marianne thinks Grandmother Borowski never let her daughter forget, it had nothing to do with work experience.

"When I was growing up," Grandmother Borowski would say, "we didn't have toilet paper. We wiped with newspaper. Can you imagine?"

"Lucky for us," Marianne's mother would say, "that Daddy thought to buy that old, used-car emporium."

"New and used now. Never forget, young lady, that he sells new cars too."

And Grandmother Borowski worked as a bagger in the grocery store. Like mother, like daughter. What goes around, comes around.

When Marianne has a baby girl she won't ever let her work at the A&P. Even if she wants to. Even if she begs to be able to bag at checkout number seven. Gets down on her hands and knees and her cobalt-blue eyes fill with tears and begs, *oh, Mama, pleeeaassseeee.*

Sleeping with Leroy is, of course, a way to get back at her mother and her dead grandmother. It's too bad they can't know about it, really, but every time Leroy puts his tongue in her mouth or touches her down there with his greasy fingers, a slow pulse of heated and displaced satisfaction moves through Marianne's every muscle until she is wet and ready for him. Begging for him, actually (a small fact that shames her afterwards). She finds it addictive. In fact, she can't get enough. Each thrust is a pin in the maternal voodoo doll of her mind.

Leroy always cries. It's enough to make Marianne sick.

Of course it wasn't called the A&P back when Marianne's mother worked there, it was called Mama Borelli's Supermarket and had a picture of a cow and a pig on the sign. They sold meat and fruit and vegetables, and plenty of homemade pasta. They sold pies. Fresh-baked.

Now Marianne bags a boxed pie, the thin see-through plastic cover steamed up with condensation from the heat outside. She's noticed lately that she often gets the same customers. She doesn't know if they come for her bagging, or for Mrs. Mabel's fast checkout fingers on the computer, her scanning abilities—but she likes to think they care if their eggs are on the bottom or on the top. Wouldn't she, Marianne thinks, if she was a purchaser of food?

Sometimes Marianne feels as if she's moving through liquid nitrogen. She feels slow and silver, spread out but fully formed.

Sarah-Jean waves from her position as she waits for the next item to come down the chute and into her bag. That's what seems to happen: The vegetable is rung through and Sarah-Jean catches it and throws it in, no matter what's below—broccoli on top of hamburger buns, for example. Marianne imagines the customer at home trying to shape a burger into something that will fit the mangled bun.

"After," Sarah-Jean shouts out at Marianne, "do you want to go to the beach?"

That's just another example of what Marianne hates about working here, about Sarah-Jean, about Leroy and Mrs. Mabel (no matter what her skill), about Charlie Folks. She hates the scream-ing conversations that go on throughout a shift. One checker to another, "What's the price on this item?" "The code. What's the code?" "Yeah, so I was at the mall the other day and there were these tank tops that were to die for." Marianne wishes for a trance-like, meditative atmosphere at work, one in which there is nothing but the bleep of the scanner, the ka-ching of the cash register, the slow, rumbling hum of the ceiling fans, and the buzz of the air con-ditioner. People glide past with quiet, smooth movements, as if they are wearing figure skates.

"Sure," Marianne says. Sarah-Jean is about to open her big mouth again and shout. "Sure. The beach sounds great."

Marianne sighs. Her grandmother never let her mother forget that she suffered as a bagger for her summer down the hill, while Marianne's mother was a fancy-girl checker. She would bring it up at Sunday dinners, martini raised in one hand, gold-coloured cigarette in the other.

"Belinda, darling," Grandmother would say. "You don't know anything about hard work. Nothing about working your fingers to the bone."

And Belinda Borowski would counter with the fact that she worked for one year at the store while her mother only worked one summer.

"All in all," Grandmother would shout, "all in all it added up to the same. But I stood at the end of the line and you, you sat on the high stool and punched numbers in."

Marianne wishes she drank martinis and smoked gold cigarettes. After her grandmother died of cirrhosis of the liver and
lung cancer (which one came first, no one seemed to know, partly
because, by the time the end came, it really didn't matter) the house
became smoke- and drink-free. Marianne's parents had found the
Lord and He said they couldn't have fun.

Another reason she'd love to break the Leroy scandal to them—
The Lord. If only she had guts. Marianne looks down at her stomach while she bags the meat separately so it doesn't leak on the
toilet paper. She pokes her guts.

Marianne's mother has Marianne's whole future all planned
out. After her daughter's brief stint with the common folks she
will come back up the hill and marry Freddie Tourniquet, Jr. He
will eventually take over his father's business, letting poor old
Fred Tourniquet, Sr. get some much-needed rest and relaxation,
and Marianne and Freddie will buy a nice house high above the
water. They will produce two delightful children. A boy and a girl.
It doesn't matter in what order. Like her mother and grandmother
before her, Marianne will hold memberships at the country club,
the Sandy Cove Marina, the Golf and Cricket Club. She will get a
weekly facial and manicure at Helga's.

The only wrench in the plan, according to Belinda, as she sits
by the pool at the Golf and Cricket Club this Thursday afternoon,
sipping Perrier (wishing deep inside, so deep she doesn't even know
she's wishing, that she could have a gin and tonic), is that her selfish
daughter claims not to love Freddie Tourniquet, Jr.

"Damn her," Belinda would like to say, but she's sworn off
swearing.

Belinda turns to her left and sees said Freddie dive off the high
board into the water, a gaggle of girls giggling around him. He
moves his powerful arms through the water and comes up like a
merman, streaming wet and looking like sex personified. Of course,
the only other wrench is Susie Malkin. That blonde girl throws
herself, throws her big-breasted, long-legged self, on Freddie and

he takes her down into the water and kisses her. Belinda doesn't believe in arranged marriages, but really, Freddie and Marianne have been together since they were babies. It's natural. It's fate. Certainly not arranged. Why, Fred, Sr. and whatever wife he is sporting presently are the Borowskis' best friends.

"Finish off," Sarah-Jean says. She is standing at the end of checkout seven, right next to Marianne. She is carrying her beach bag and is dressed in shorts and a T-shirt. Marianne knows Sarah-Jean's uniform is hanging on the back of the employees' washroom door like it is every day. Stinky. She never takes it home to get washed. Marianne's housekeeper starches hers. Presses it. Every morning it's fresh-smelling and stiff. "Finish off and let's get out of here."

Marianne stops bagging, gives her empty bags to Tracy for the next shift and glides back into the washroom to change. She emerges wearing a summer dress, her suit underneath. Sarah-Jean is in the parking lot with Leroy. She is leaning on his car and smoking a cigarette. For a moment Marianne watches them through the window.

"You don't want to hang out with them," Charlie Folks says, stepping up to her. "Go see your people at the club. Go swimming there. That's where you belong."

Marianne isn't sure she heard that correctly. She looks at Charlie and he's smiling pleasantly. He's old. Simple-minded. He meant nothing by it, she's sure. My people, Marianne thinks. What an odd thing to say. She walks out the door towards Leroy and Sarah-Jean and says, "Let's go to the beach."

It is the moments underwater that Marianne treasures. The moments when, at the crowded, filthy beach, she is finally alone. Everything is muted. Sound echoes softly, water rushes around her, comforting her. Cleaning her. Cleaning off the smell of sour milk, the iron stench of meat, the rotten egg.

Sarah-Jean sitting up on the sand wondering, wondering.

"Where's Marianne?" Leroy asks.

"In the water."

They've spread their towels together in three straight rows and Sarah-Jean kicks a bit of sand on Marianne's pink one. Leroy watches, but says nothing.

"She's going to drown," he says.

"The lifeguard will save her. She does this every day. For attention. It's all about attention."

That's what Sarah-Jean's mother said to her just before she left. Sarah-Jean was six years old and she can still vaguely remember what her mother looked like, even after her father destroyed all the photos with his cigarette lighter. "You just need too much attention," she had said. Sarah-Jean, crouched on the stairwell, looking down at the woman's receding form, her father grabbing hold of an arm, a coat, a hem. And then her mother was gone. Her mother was her father's whipping post and when she left, Sarah-Jean stepped up to the plate.

Sarah-Jean's got bruises on her arms and legs that she explains away to others as the speed of her bagging at checkout number five.

"Always bumping into things. Speedy Gonzalez," she says.

"I'm going to go out and get her," Leroy says. "I need me some."

"Some what?"

"Don't be stupid."

"You can get some here. You know that."

"I'll do that," Leroy says and then whistles. "When I run out of what she has to offer."

Sarah-Jean helped Leroy save up to buy his car. She walked to school with him every day. Sometimes he pulls her father off of her when, in a drunken rage, he's taken hold of her hair, her leg, her shoe, and is pulling, squeezing, beating. But Leroy has a short-term memory, or a one-focus memory—namely, for Marianne. Nothing but Marianne clouding his milky grey eyes, his dumbbell head, those ears sticking out like weights. Fuck him, Sarah-Jean thinks.

Marianne stands waist-high in the water. She's clean. She's baptized. She's free of the pressures of the world. And then she sees

Leroy bearing down on her. Skinny boy. His ears at right angles to his head. He's rushing through the water, tossing it over the kids who are swimming shallow, and heading towards her like a shark after a surfboard. Marianne cowers slightly.

"Hey, baby."

Marianne nods. All the clean feeling has gone. Now she's back in the real world with dirty old Leroy and Sarah-Jean. When she should be up at the country club. Up there, sipping things, watching tanned bodies swimming, noting the cleanliness around her. White-washed and nice, the smell of tangerine and coconut in the air.

Marianne thinks being born rich isn't as easy as it sounds. There are expectations and demands made upon you that are sometimes out of this world. And the only way to rebel is to go down, get filthy.

Leroy crashes into her.

Then Sarah-Jean comes in too and they are a crowd of three in the water up to their waists. Marianne watches a chocolate bar wrapper float past.

"Let's go to the sand dunes," Leroy says. He whines it, although he tries not to.

"Not today, Leroy," Marianne says.

"You two just want to … you know … fuck. That's all you ever want to do," Sarah-Jean says.

"Yeah?" Leroy says. "What's wrong with that?"

"Well, it gets pretty boring for me."

"Come on, baby." Leroy has his hands on Marianne's stomach, her ass, her back. "Come on."

Marianne thinks it's like having a dog under the dinner table. Begging, scratching, crying, panting. Boys and dogs. One and the same.

Just before Grandmother Borowski died she confessed to Mari-anne she had been involved in a long-standing love affair with the man who wrapped gifts at the Fashion Boutique in the mall. His station in life was so low that Grandmother Borowski felt as if she were the Queen of England when she lay next to him. His *gonna*s and his *ain't*s. His rough hands that never saw a manicure.

The fruit, Marianne thinks, never falls far from the tree. And just as she's thinking this, just as she's thinking there are only a couple more weeks of this summer left and then she'll be back up on the hill living the life everyone wants her to live so she might as well head off to the sand dunes with Leroy, just as an image of her bronzing by the pool at the country club comes into her head, chubby Sarah-Jean punches her in the face and, to make matters worse, Freddie Tourniquet, Jr., drunk and loud, drives into the beach parking lot with a Mercedes-Benz full of Marianne's status-type *friends*. Coming down to visit the lower class, the poor, Marianne thinks just as she receives a fistful from Sarah-Jean and her nose begins to spout blood. Leroy is amazed. Later, he reasons, he's amazed because Marianne's blood is the same colour as his. He assumed somehow it would be royal purple. But, for now, he's just stunned Sarah-Jean has punched Marianne Borowski.

And then pandemonium breaks out. Freddie, in his alcohol-induced state, and secretly aware of his pseudo-arranged marriage status (really, he does covet Marianne, even though Susie Malkin has nicer legs and has been plenty of fun this summer), sees Marianne in the water, her nose leaking blood, staring shockingly at that freaky-looking kid with the big head and crazy ears who sometimes sells him drugs by the Marina. One plus one equals two, in Freddie's head, and so he assumes the asshole has struck his soon-to-be wife. (The fact Freddie has spent the summer ignoring Marianne because her lowly job makes him look bad doesn't faze him one bit. He knows he'll get her back once she's been positioned comfortably up on the hill again, once she never has to go down the hill for anything.)

Later, after the waves die down and Sarah-Jean has run up to grab her towel to cover her topless state, after Leroy has lit up a cigarette and puffed sulkily through swollen, bleeding lips, much later, everyone looks around for Marianne Borowski. They begin calling for her, searching the beach, the water for her. The whole gang (minutes ago they were beating the crap out of each other) is now working together as one. A group of half-bloodied, swollen, bruised teenagers, all moving up and down the beach calling, "Marianne? Marianne?" What's particularly interesting about this is the togetherness of the people. Up-the-hill people searching with down-the-hill people. Down-the-hill people helping up-the-hill people over the sand dunes.

In this way, although it accomplishes nothing, Marianne has the final say. Pity that, every summer, in every watery town all over the world, there is at least one drowning.

In this way, Marianne confirms her love of space, and still learns nothing about speed.

Off in the distance, far, far away, Marianne swims out of sight. She swims until she gets too tired to swim and then, like a rock, she sinks.

Dogs

The dog is poised in the snow, alert, ready to jump.

"Jump," Eric says.

The dog jumps over the ramp Eric has created out of snow.

"Good boy."

After writing these sentences, the woman stares at herself in the mirror in front of her desk. She put the mirror up to make the room look less crowded, to give the room a sense of depth and space that really isn't there. The mirror doesn't work, though. The mirror only makes the woman stare at her reflection and think about the fact that she is aging. She sees her chins—yes, chins—in the mirror. She sees the bags under her eyes. Her dull hair. Mostly, though, the woman sees the set of her jaw, the way her face has become almost square, her jaw clenched tight.

The woman says to herself, "I look manly." Then, because she is talking to herself and feeling nervous about it, because she catches her reflection with mouth open, yapping, and no one else in the small room, she turns to her dog, who is under her rolling desk chair within inches of getting his tail run over, and she smiles at her dog as if she had intended to say that last comment to her dog. Not to herself. In the mirror.

The dog looks up at the woman. Idolatry. He adores her. The woman knows there will never be any person on earth who will adore her the way this dog does and so she reaches down and pats his head. Then she rolls her chair back from the desk and the dog yelps because she has rolled over his tail.

Eric is proud of his new dog, which is a before-Christmas present from his mostly absent father. The dog is a terrier and the card his father included with the dog said that his breed kills rats. Eric doesn't think they have any rats in Toronto, but he isn't sure. He is sure they have plenty of raccoons because his mother is always shouting at them when they get into the garbage cans. Eric shakes his head because the raccoons don't speak English, they speak Raccoon. The dog crouches down in the snow again, ready to leap, but Eric stops the dog and builds his snow-ramp higher and the dog waits patiently.

The woman doesn't really care about dogs or ramps made out of snow or even this boy named Eric who has a mostly absent father and an angry mother.

Does she?

Tonight is the annual winter party at her in-laws' house and the woman can't think of anything but how drained and pale and awful she feels. A winter party. What is that? After Christmas, before Valentine's Day. An excuse to drive your daughter-in-law crazy. But for now, her character Eric can wait. The woman has to do something to get herself in the mood to chat with her mother-in-law.

"You'd think," the woman tells her dog (her dog who is nothing like the dog Eric has just received. Her dog is a lumbering, old yellow Lab. He smells. He farts. His farts smell. His drool drips on the floor and leaves marks on the shiny hardwood. But he's her dog and she often feels as if she loves him in a way she doesn't love her husband or her children, or definitely her mother-in-law). "You'd think that just one year I'd be in the mood to go to this party," the woman says to her dog. "Just one year. Out of fifteen years. Surely there should be one year I'd like to go and hang out with the in-laws and drink wine and smile and be cheery."

Maybe, the woman thinks, her face wouldn't be so stiff-jawed if she tried to have a good time at these things. Maybe she wouldn't be getting square-faced, masculine, aged.

The dog wags his tail. The tail she ran over. It's still attached. That's good, the woman thinks.

Then the husband comes into the woman's office. He talks to her, standing behind her desk, while he studies his reflection in the mirror. The woman notes that he's quite handsome still. His face has become as angular as her face is, but of course this works on a man.

"What are you doing?" the husband asks.

The dog's tail thumps wildly on the floor. Two people he loves in the same room at the same time. The dog must wonder, the woman thinks, if he has died and gone to heaven. Maybe, the dog must think, his tail injury has killed him.

"I'm writing a story."

"Oh." The husband turns his face a bit to the side to check out his profile.

"Do you mind?"

"What?"

"What did you want? Did you want something?"

"No. I just wondered what you were doing."

"Well, I'm trying to write a story."

The husband smiles at himself. The woman notes that he is wearing the sweater his mother bought him for Christmas this year. A point for him, the woman thinks. A point for the husband. She wonders if she has anything that her mother-in-law has given her lately that she still fits into. Something she could wear to the winter party. The woman contemplates this, her fingers lightly touching the computer keyboard.

"What's your story about?"

"A boy and his new dog."

"Oh," the husband says. He sounds disappointed.

"What do you mean, oh?"

"Well, what do the boy and the dog do?"

"Things, okay. Things. They do things."

The husband backs out of the room. "I was just wondering, that's all."

"Look," the woman says. She sighs. "I haven't got much time. We have to go to this stupid party. And I haven't written a lot lately. Not in a long time. I need to write something. Or I won't have a good time at the party."

The husband looks astonished.

The dog sits, haunches on the floor. The woman puts her hand down and pats the dog.

"Okay, that's fine. I'll leave you alone."

"Yes, thank you."

Dogs

Eric and his dog play in the snow all afternoon.
Sometimes Eric stops playing and looks around for
rats even though it is winter and he doesn't think
there will be rats around. There is no harm looking, Eric thinks, because he knows his dog would like
rats. After all, his dog was bred to be a rat-killer.
The dog has fun with Eric, jumping over the snow ramp
and looking for rats. Soon Eric's mother calls him in
for supper.

Shit, the woman thinks. She looks at her watch. The husband is
right. This boy and his dog, they don't do anything. Maybe, the
woman wonders, this story doesn't have anything to do with the
boy or the dog or the fact that the dog chases rats. Maybe it has
something to do with the mostly absent father. Of course that's it.
Why is he absent? And why mostly?

Eric wipes the dog's paws off, just like his mother
told him to do. She told him if he didn't wipe that
dog's paws off every time the dog came into the house
then his mother would get rid of him. Eric wasn't
sure whether she meant she'd get rid of Eric or the
dog. "Off he goes," is what she said in her huffy
way, waving her arms at him. Then she put her hands
on her hips and clenched her jaw and her furrowed
her brow. Even Eric's dog was scared. This dog who
could potentially kill sharp-fanged rats backed into
a corner.

The husband has come back into the room and is staring at the woman through the mirror.

"What? What do you want?"

"You need to get dressed," he says. "My mom expects us by five."

"Yes, yes." Jesus, the woman thinks, five o'clock.

"And are you going to get the kids ready?"

"They aren't ready yet?"

"No. I can't find Junie. I think she went over to Meg's house to play in the snow."

"Christ," the woman says. She shouts this. "Where's Shaun?"

"He's in his room," the man says.

"Get him ready then, okay? I'll be out in a minute."

A minute. Not a minute. Maybe another fifteen minutes. If she only had fifteen minutes. She could write a lot in fifteen minutes.

The scarf. That's what she'll wear. She has that scarf her mother-in-law gave her last Christmas and she's never worn it. It's not really a scarf, it's a … wrap? A *pashmina*? Is that what those things are called? It's something she can drape over her shoulders like a sophisticated woman would. In the dentist's office the other day the woman was reading a Martha Stewart magazine left on the table by someone else and it said that these things were called *pashminas*. Not wraps. Not scarves. If you're going to wear them, the magazine said, get the name right.

But she was going to wear her green dress and the wrap is green too. That will look awful. She will look like an elf. An aging, square-jawed elf. So now the woman has to think about what else she can wear so that she can wrap the stupid scarf thing around her shoulders to gain extra points from her mother-in-law.

Black dress, black dress, black dress. Surely she has a black dress.

Dogs

After wiping the dog's paws Eric lets him into the
house. The dog bolts through.…

No, the woman thinks, the dog tiptoes through the kitchen, as if he
senses the presence of the mostly absent father. She only has fifteen
minutes, the mostly absent father better come into the story quickly.

"Hello son," the father says.
  "Dad," Eric shouts, running into the kitchen and
clinging to his father.
  "Your boots!" the mother screams. She is nursing
a Scotch. She is standing in high-heeled shoes by the
kitchen sink, her thin torso wrapped in an apron even
though nothing is cooking. Her long nails are clutching her drink. "Take off your boots, Eric, or off you
go."
  Eric remembered the dog's paws, but forgot his
boots.…

(Telling, this is telling. Show this, the woman thinks).

"But I remembered the dog," Eric says, his face
flushed. "I'm sorry, I remembered the dog." He takes
off his boots and tries to wipe up the wet on the
floor with his socks. He skates over the wet. But the
mother sighs and sips her drink, her ice cubes clink-
ing against the glass.
  Eric wonders why he was called in for supper when
there is no supper.

The father still has his coat on and Eric suddenly notices his father's boots. Eric also notices the
mother says nothing about this.

"Listen, kid," the father says. "Do you like your
dog?"

Eric nods and the dog bounds excitedly around
them, jumping up against the mother's leg. The dog
jumps dangerously close to her nylons, dangerously
close to her high-heeled, pointy shoes.

"I don't like the dog," the mother says harshly.
"I think—"

"What?" the woman shouts. Her son, Shaun, is calling for her from
down the hall. He is in his bedroom and he's shouting, "Mom," as
if he's being attacked by killer bees.

"What do you want?"

The husband comes back into the woman's small office and
says, "Shaun wants to know what you want him to wear to the
party."

"Oh for God's sake," the woman says. She puts her clenched
jaw down on her desk. She thinks she might cry. Or kill someone.
"I don't care."

"You don't care?" the husband says. "Really?"

"Really."

"Mom says you can wear whatever you want." The husband
leaves the office, tiptoes out, and shuts the door behind him.

The woman understands Christmas parties. You have to get
together for Christmas with family. It's in the rule book. But a
winter party? What exactly are you celebrating? Snow? Cold? Her
mother-in-law says it's an excuse to get together in a season that is
mainly for hermiting and hibernation.

```
"I think the dog smells."
    "Honey," the mostly absent father says, laughing.
The mother holds up her glass and shakes it, indicat-
ing she wants a refill. The father goes to the liquor
cabinet.
```

"No," the woman shouts. "Wait." She jumps up from her desk. "I didn't mean you could wear anything. Shaun?"

The woman leaves her office and heads down the hall to her son's room. She opens the door. Inside the husband and her son are sitting on the floor playing dominoes. The son is wearing stained track pants and a sweater that is two sizes too big. His hair is sticking up.

"No, no, no."

"I told you," the boy says to the husband. "I told you that she didn't mean that."

The woman pauses. "What do you mean, Shaun?"

Shaun says nothing. The husband gets up from the floor. "Come on. Let's get you in something presentable."

"It's your mother, for God's sake. It's her winter party," the woman says. "Your mother."

"Yeah, I know. I just thought." The husband pauses.

"What? That she suddenly wouldn't care what her grandchildren were wearing? That suddenly she thought that just seeing her grandchildren was more important than what they were wearing? Ha." The woman is shrill. She knows her voice is shrill and she tries to lower it. "This is, after all, your mother."

"I just thought." The husband doesn't complete his sentence. The woman realizes, all of a sudden, that the husband rarely completes his sentences. He says half of something and then stops. This infuriates her. It has always angered her, given her a square jaw, but just now she put a shape around it, identified it. He often doesn't finish his sentences.

The dog knocks over the dominoes. The woman's son yells at the dog. "Bad dog. Bad, bad dog." The boy hits the dog lightly on his rump. The dog cowers.

"Don't hit the dog," the woman says. "That's not nice."

"I haven't found Junie yet," the husband says. "Have you seen—"

"But you always hit the dog," the boy says.

The woman turns from where she was heading out the boy's bedroom door. She looks at the husband. At the boy. At the sad dog. "And," she says, "I see you've been looking hard for her?"

"Well."

"Well?"

Why, the woman thinks, does she always sound like this?

"We have to leave in half an hour," the husband says, sheepishly. "I'll call Meg's house again. She might be—"

"Or you could walk over and get her? She has to get dressed too, you know."

"Or I could help Shaun here and you could walk.... Or maybe...?" The husband stops talking when he sees the woman's face.

Back in the kitchen the mother is in the process of getting profoundly drunk. She is tottering in those high heels and almost falling over. The mostly absent father is looking at his watch. He is petting the incredibly hyper, rat-chasing, terrier dog. Eric is wondering if he'll get supper tonight. Whenever his mother gets drunk his father says he has to go somewhere and he leaves and doesn't come back for a long time. And it's almost Christmas and the mother's Scotch bottle is almost empty and the father still hasn't taken off his coat or boots. Outside the snow-ramp is slowly being covered with a fresh dusting of icy whiteness. Eric can see it through the window. When he chooses to lift his eyes from the floor and when he chooses to look past his mother and out into the gradual evening he sees his snow-ramp disappearing.

Here, in the kitchen, Eric's father suddenly stands.

"No," Eric shouts. "Sit."

His father sits. The dog sits.

"What did you say to him?" the mother shouts, holding out her long-nailed pointy finger. She stabs at the air. "Did you say sit?"

"What are you going to name the dog, son?" the father asks.

"I'm not sure."

"What?" the mother says. "I can't hear anything. Everything is so quiet that I can't hear a thing." She leans into the sink and then slides down a bit, off her heels. She crouches on the floor and Eric can see her nylon stockings at the top where they join between her legs. He can see an oval part there that is darker than the nylons on her legs. "These shoes are too high," she says.

"I think we need more Scotch," the father says and he stands to leave.

"No," Eric says again. "Sit."

The dog sits but this time Eric's father doesn't.

Outside the woman's office doors everything is silent. Eerily.

She wonders first if her story is sounding too much like a Raymond Carver story. Then she wonders if maybe her family left without her. Which wouldn't be too bad, she supposes. She stands and looks out the little window in her room and out to the street. There they are. Junie and Shaun and the husband. There they are, in the snow, looking happy with each other. Shaun is laughing. The woman sees Shaun is wearing something on his legs other than grey track pants. That's a start, she thinks. And Junie looks like she's brushed her hair. The woman can see a hairclip shining in the dimming light. She looks at her watch. If they were to leave, the woman would have to be ready in five minutes. She would have to somehow put on nylons, heels, a black dress (does she even have one?), jewellery, perfume, brush her hair, apply lipstick and foundation and eyeshadow and mascara, and wrap that damn green shawl/ *pashmina* thing around her shoulders. She would have to do all that and then head down the stairs and out the front door and into the car where the husband would drive them all for half an hour through the city and out to her in-laws' house. There would be half a dozen cars in the driveway (a few trucks, vans), the house would glow with heat and cheer and smell of food. Her mother-in-law, well, she would peck the woman on the cheek and grab dangerously at Shaun and Junie, wanting to touch and hug.

First one glass of wine, or whatever it is they are serving (Scotch?), and then another. Smile. Laugh. Toast the winter season.

What's wrong with that? the woman thinks. What's wrong with this picture? This story?

The husband looks up and sees the woman at her office window. He points her out to the children and they all start to wave madly, laughing and waving and throwing their arms up in the air at her, their mother, as she stands stiffly looking down on them. Her son then throws a snowball and, of course, Junie follows suit. Then the husband throws one and it hits the office window right at where her forehead is. *Smack.* She ducks.

The husband below ducks too, as if he expects her to come flying out through the window and into the dusk, arms flailing wildly, tearing at him in a rage. As if he expects her to be mad.

But she isn't. The woman actually laughs. She can't help herself. The husband looked so scared. She claps her hands. They continue to throw snow.

Dogs

And then the husband looks at his watch, points to it, looks at her. Mouths, *are you ready?*

```
The dog's name, Eric decides later, after his father
has left the house promising to come back shortly,
after his mother passed out on the kitchen floor, her
underwear showing, her drink spilled beside her,
after the dog lapped up the drink and then burped
continuously in front of the TV and then fell into a
deep slumber and snored heartily beside Eric as he
lay in bed, his stomach rumbling, hungry for supper,
the dog's name is.…
```

Is what? The woman does not know. And, although it is important to the whole feeling of the story, to the ending of the story, to Eric's future and his past, to whether or not this is a successful story, the woman doesn't know the name. Not now. Now she has run two pairs of nylons with her jagged fingernails, her winter-chapped hands, and she is rushing to put on her last pair. She has puffed up her hair. She has somehow got rid of the bags under her eyes and put perfume behind her ears.

"Are you coming? It's time…," the husband shouts from the front door. "Hurry up. I think we should—"

"I'm coming, I'm coming," the woman says. "Just wait. Wait for me."

Don't leave, the woman thinks. But she knows they won't leave her there, by herself. She knows that no matter what, they won't ever leave her alone and go to a party without her.

Even if it's a party she doesn't want to go to.

The dog, though, her soft yellow Lab named Poodle, they will all leave him. And he will get into the dying flowers on the dining

163

room table. The ones the husband brought home spontaneously a week ago, saying, "I thought you'd...." Poodle will eat all of them. The roses. The daffodils. The baby's breath. Everything. He will drink the water. And then he will lie under the dining room table with a stomach that feels as if someone has planted a bomb inside of it and detonated that bomb, his stomach in shreds and pieces inside of him, and he will burp and fart and drool and groan—because, really, what else can he do?—until the family comes home, happy and laughing and smelling of food and drink and good cheer.

Just Like Rain

A ndy's father comes in on the 2:02 a.m. bus from outside of the city. Andy makes it to the bus station at 2 a.m. He sits on the bench outside the terminal doors smoking a cigarette and waiting. It is July, the middle of a hot summer, one of the hottest, driest summers Andy can remember.

"Hey there," his father says when he sees him. "You look horrible."

Andy smiles and takes his father's outstretched hand. "Just tired, that's all."

"And a little drunk, I'd say." His father laughs.

Andy's father is a small man. Short and thin with wiry, old-man, bow legs. He is wearing Bermuda shorts and a button-up dress shirt with long sleeves. The fashion statement is odd and Andy can't help but stare.

"I hopped on the bus right after my shift," Andy's father says, noticing his son glancing at his clothing. "Didn't have time to do anything but take my pants off." He laughs. His laugh is like a bark. He coughs and spits phlegm on the ground.

Andy lights another cigarette. He isn't in a hurry to get anywhere soon. And his father is right. Andy is a little drunk. He needs to sit on the bench for a while, soak in the mild coolness of the night, get his bearings, before he does anything else.

Andy's father's been sitting in the bus for four hours and is ready to do anything but sit again.

"Let's go now," he says. "Let's get a move on."

But Andy sucks on his cigarette and looks down the empty street, past the huge shopping mall, towards the city.

"In a minute," he says. "I need to rest a bit first."

Andy's father paces up and down in front of the terminal building, reading all the posters stuck on the walls.

"Free concert in the park on Thursday," he shouts. "Two-fer-one night at Combo's tomorrow. Would you look at that."

Andy looks down at the small suitcase his father has placed by his feet. It is worn almost thin from travel, from being banged and bumped around on buses. There are stickers holding tears together, stickers so old Andy can't make out the words. Silver duct tape wrapped around and around the handle makes for a more comfortable hold.

Andy's father sits down next to his son and places a thin arm around his shoulders. "Okay, enough resting," he says. "I'm ready to go now."

Andy is much taller than his father. More like his mother than his father. He has high cheekbones and longish, black hair. He is thin, though, and this thinness is what brings him closer to his father in appearance. His mother was heavy and solid, round but firm. Andy remembers when he used to pretend-punch his mother in the stomach and she would take the small blows with her hips pushed out and her stomach sucked in. His hand would practically bounce back off her flesh and he likened it to punching Silly Putty.

Andy gets up off the bench, shrugging his father's arm off his shoulders, and stretches. "It's been a long couple of months, Dad."

Andy's father looks down the street and puts a hand up to shade his eyes. "Streetlights are bright in the city, aren't they?" He laughs.

Andy picks up his father's suitcase and starts walking towards the parking lot, towards his truck. His is the only truck in the lot, the rest of the vehicles are foreign and small and bright in colour. His truck is silver, tinged with rust. There is a dent in the rear fender and it's missing a tail light.

Andy's father walks quickly behind him and opens the truck door and hops in. Andy never locks the doors of his truck. Why would anyone want to steal it?

Andy throws the suitcase, much lighter than it looks, into the back of the truck and slides in behind the wheel.

"What if it rains?" his father asks. "My bag'll get wet."

"Won't rain," Andy says. "It hasn't rained in weeks."

"But what if it does?"

Andy gets out of the truck, grabs his father's suitcase and puts it on the seat between them. His father pats the bag soothingly, strokes the mangled vinyl as he would a sleeping cat.

"There was a funny man sitting with me on the bus," he says. He laughs. The barking sound startles Andy. For a minute he thinks his truck has backfired as he starts it up.

"Yeah?"

"Yeah. He was wearing this hairpiece that just kept falling forward. Said he'd run out of glue or something. And he smelled bad. Boy did he smell. No one else would sit with him."

"Yeah?"

"Yeah."

Andy pulls the truck out of the lot and heads down the deserted streets of the city slowly, looking around at the stores as if he'd just now arrived there.

"He said his name was Stevens. You know him?"

"No."

"You sure now? He was a big fellow. Built like a truck. Rough around the edges. Had no shine, really. Except his head." Andy's father laughs again. He slaps his knee with one hand. The other hand is still patting the suitcase.

"You want to go see her now?" Andy asks.

"Maybe."

"Maybe yes or maybe no?"

"Just maybe."

There is silence inside the truck. Andy rubs a hand through his hair. He hasn't had a cut in months. Soon he'll be wearing a ponytail. Soon he'll look like a girl. The feel of the Kahlúa and milk he had before he came is wearing off and now he's just headachy and tired with a sloppy, dirty taste in his mouth. He doesn't know why he had to drink to pick up his father. It's just a habit from the past.

Andy's girlfriend, Sue, is waiting for him in her bed right now. He thinks she's probably sitting up with the TV on, a blanket wrapped around her legs. Or maybe she's sleeping.

"Maybe yes, I guess."

"Now?"

Andy's father looks at him. "That Stevens guy said he knew you. Said everyone in this city knows you." He laughs. "Just trying to make me proud, I guess."

"No one knows me, Dad. This is a big city. This isn't like your home."

"Where's my home?" Andy's father looks out the window as they drive slowly through the city. "It's raining," he says. "I told you it would rain."

"It's not raining."

"The street's wet."

Andy looks down at the street. It is, indeed, wet. "The cleaner's been by."

"Cleaner?"

"The streets get cleaned at night."

"Shit," his father says. Loud air escapes through his nose. "Cleaning the streets. What next?"

"We'll just go see her then."

"It's been a while, son," Andy's father says. "It's been a long while."

"I know, Dad."

"What'll I say?"

"You'll think of something."

They are quiet as Andy drives the rest of the way. Andy imagines things in his mind. Like the police pulling him over and charging him with drunk driving. Like Sue having sex with other men. Like his mother's tight stomach as he pretend-punched it. Like his father's rundown house in the country, surrounded by fields of wild grass and a stream where he washes his old face every morning. Andy thinks about these things until he pulls into the hospital parking lot and pays the attendant.

"Ten dollars?" Andy's father says. He lets his breath out in astonishment. "Ten dollars to park?"

Andy smiles. "Wait until you see how much coffee costs in the city."

"And you wonder why I don't visit here."

Andy's never wondered why his father has never visited. He's been wondering more, lately, in the last six hours since his father's phone call, about why he is here.

The two men, one short and thin, the other tall and thin, twenty-seven years between them, get out of the truck and shut the doors behind them in unison. The joint bang sounds like a gunshot in the quiet, hot air. Andy jumps a bit on the balls of his feet. His father starts walking towards the hospital, his suitcase in hand.

"You can leave your bag, Dad."

"I'd rather not."

Andy jogs a little to catch up to his father.

They enter the hospital through Emergency and Andy talks to the woman behind the front desk. A security guard looks into

Andy's father's suitcase and then lets them through into the waiting room.

"A nurse will take you there," the woman behind the counter says. "Just you wait now."

"What's going on?" whispers Andy's father.

"They've got tight security here," Andy says. "Something to do with newborn babies and stuff. All the drugs they've got here, I guess. Normally they won't let you in at this time, visiting hours and all. I got special permission..." Andy stops talking.

Andy's father looks confused.

"I'm going to go out and smoke," Andy says. "You can stay here."

But Andy's father clutches his suitcase to his chest and follows his son out again into the night. They stand beside the security guard and Andy smokes. Soon a heavy-set man in white pants and shirt comes out and taps Andy on the shoulder.

"You can follow me now," he says.

"That's a nurse?" Andy's father laughs. "In my day..." he begins, but then notices Andy's expression and stops talking.

The nurse takes them to the bank of elevators and they stand together silently watching the numbers light up above the doors.

"What'll I say?" asks Andy's father.

Andy shrugs. "Why are you here?"

Andy's father looks at him. Straight up at his son. "To see the city," he says. He laughs. The nurse smiles.

Andy thinks that Sue will soon be mad he drank all her milk with his Kahlúa, but it was the only thing to drink in the apartment and he couldn't drink it straight because it was much too sweet. Sue'll be looking for the milk to have on her cereal and it'll be gone. And she has to go to work so she'll have no time to get milk that quickly or that early. She'll be so mad that she might not let him sleep over again for a while. And right now in his life Andy needs all the sleeping-over, all the warm-body-in-bed nights he can get. He wants to snuggle into something these days, and it doesn't really matter what, something he can hold onto tightly and not let go. He needs a solid back to wrap his arms around. A warm back. A woman's back.

They get off the elevator and walk down the hall side by side.

"Maybe you'd like to come visit me in the country," Andy's father says suddenly. He stops walking and looks at his suitcase. "Come see my house again. I've fixed it up some since you were last there. And I've got myself a good job now." He points to his long-sleeved dress shirt as if that explains everything.

"Come on." Andy wants to get back to Sue's apartment before she leaves for her shift at the factory. He wants to explain to her why he had to sit alone at her kitchen table and drink.

But Andy's father doesn't want to move. He stands there, unmoving. "I don't know," he says, quietly.

"Are you coming?" asks the nurse.

"In a minute."

Andy takes his father's arm and starts to tug him a bit. "Let's go." It surprises Andy that his father can hold his stance, considering he's so thin and weak-looking.

"I don't know if I can see her," Andy's father says.

"Then why'd you come?"

"I don't know."

"Shit."

Andy's father walks over to a window and looks out. "It looks like rain on the streets, doesn't it?" he says. "All wet and shiny like that."

"Dad."

"Are you two coming? I have things to do," the nurse says. He is standing with his arms crossed in front of his large belly.

Andy thinks of how his father will be amazed at the sight of his mother. All that flesh now gone.

"Come on, Dad. Let's just get it over with and I'll drop you off at my place and you can sleep there."

"Hmm?" Andy's father is staring out the window. "Just like rain," he mumbles.

"I'll go see her, then," Andy says to the nurse.

"We can't leave him here," the nurse says. "He'll have to come at least to the door of the room."

Andy's father turns to his son and the nurse. "I'll wait for you outside of her room," he says.

They walk together again.

The nurse leaves them at the room and walks over to the nurse's station where he can do some paperwork and still keep an eye on the two men.

"Crazy old guy," Andy hears the nurse say to another nurse on duty. Andy watches her look up from the book she is reading and nod.

"Him?"

"Yeah." Andy's nurse picks up a pen and writes something in a large three-ring binder. He yawns.

"Are you coming in?" Andy asks his father.

"I'll sit here for a while," Andy's father says, motioning to a chair in the hall. Andy starts to walk into his mother's room when his father's hand shoots out and grabs his wrist. The suitcase falls to the floor.

"Hey," Andy says.

"I haven't seen her in years," Andy's father says. "Has she changed any?" He holds on tight to Andy's wrist.

Andy laughs. He can't help himself. "Not much," he says, thinking about her shrunken-apple face, her thin arms stuck with needles, her hacking, wheezing voice, the skin draping off her like tent flaps. "Not much at all." Andy turns to face his father. He looks down at his father's hand on his wrist. "I can't help but wonder," he says "what it is you are really doing here. I mean"—Andy pauses—"it's been so long. You just up and left and we haven't seen you in years, and now, out of the blue, you call me and come into the city to see her. Why?"

"You remember my house?" Andy's father asks. "In the country?"

Andy nods. He remembers how worn-looking it was. He remembers how his father would throw the food garbage out the window for the raccoons to eat. He remembers that he wanted to take a bus home as soon as he walked in the door and he remembers that he spent the whole week there wondering why his mother would send him away, send him to visit someone he didn't even know, in the first place.

"You remember the stream out back?"

"Yeah." Andy yawns. He can't help himself.

"Well, the stream has dried up." His father looks at the floor, still clutching Andy's wrist.

"Yeah, so?"

"It just dried up. A couple of weeks ago."

Andy can hear his mother stirring in her bed. Their voices have woken her.

"So what, Dad? What's that have to do with anything?"

No matter how hard he tries to remember a time when the three of them lived together, Andy can't. It's just not part of his memories. He can remember his mom with her thick skin, her rosy cheeks, her deep laugh. He can remember jumping into her bed when he was a little boy and holding her large face in his small hands and kissing her nose. "Wake up, sleepyhead," he'd say and she would roll away from him, smiling, so he could wrap his small body up against her back and hold on.

"I just thought it was time I see her again," Andy's father says.

"Well, go see her then." Andy steps back from the door. He takes his father's stiff hand off his wrist. "Go see her."

"What about my suitcase?"

"I'll hold your suitcase."

"What'll I say?"

Andy thinks for a bit. He hears his mother coughing in her room. She groans. "Tell her about the stream drying up," he says. "Or tell her whatever you want. I don't care, really."

And, as Andy's father enters the room quietly, his head down, his eyes focused on the floor, Andy sits in the chair outside of the room and holds on tight to his father's small, vinyl suitcase. He holds on to the suitcase and he thinks of how little his father carries when he has had to travel so far.

The Good Little Girl

She hates the way this night has turned out. Crouched now behind the car in the driveway of a house she doesn't recognize, Missy feels the ache in her knees. Skinned, when she ran away from him. Both knees are bleeding, she's sure of it, and her mother will ask her what happened and then kill her. It's dark, even with the streetlights scattered here and there down the neighbourhood. She can't see anything but the fender of the car, the licence plate, the night around her. She can hear him, though, as he walks down the street, the clip-clop of his hard shoes on the empty pavement. All noise swells—crickets chirping, his shoes, a car turning the corner two blocks away, his shoes, a dog barking in the house behind her, his shoes, her breath. She swears she can hear the click of the streetlight on the corner as it turns from red to green. Green means go. Should she go? His shoes, she hears his shoes pounding in her head. He's walking slower now.

"Come out, come out, wherever you are."

His voice.

His shoes.

Her breath and blood and heartbeat. Everything is so loud she wants to scream. The dog won't stop barking in the house behind her. Whose house? Missy doesn't know. She ran as fast as she could, left Emily and Susan behind, and bolted in the direction of Emily's house. She thought she would get away from him, that he would chase the other girls, but instead he came after her.

"It's supposed to be fun," Missy says to her mother earlier in the day before the sleepover party. "Emily says we're going to sleep in her parents' trailer."

"Why?"

"It's in their carport. Parked right there. It won't move."

"What if it rolls?" Missy's mother isn't interested. She is smoking, holding a glass of wine, and watching TV. All at the same time.

"It won't roll."

"Don't jump up and down or it might," her mother says. She butts out her cigarette and looks straight at Missy. "And be good. You're too young to be bad."

"I'm not bad."

"That's what I'm saying."

"What are you saying?"

"Oh, Miss," her mother sighs. "You know what I'm saying."

It's the old don't-be-like-me talk. Missy's heard it a thousand times. Don't smoke or drink or do drugs. Don't have sex with older boys. And especially—don't get pregnant. You don't want a little girl named Missy asking you if she can go to a sleepover in her friend's parents' trailer, do you? When you are only twenty-nine years old and your daughter is twelve. My God. Who wants that? And then you'd end up working at Walmart for nine dollars an hour, and hanging out at the bars after because no one at Walmart is worth dating. No one at the bars is either, according to Missy's mom, who only brings them home for the night and never sees them again.

Missy thinks this is a typical story. A boring story. She's heard it over and over again all her life. Yes, I'm sorry I was born, Missy thinks. I'm sorry I wrecked your life. It had such potential. You were going to be so much more. What? Missy never finds out. Her mother never gets that far.

But she loves her mom, even when she gives her that *don't wreck your life* speech. Because being twenty-nine years old, her mom is certainly better-looking and more fun than most of her friends' moms. Sometimes it's like having a big sister. Soon Missy will fit into her mom's clothes and then she'll have two whole wardrobes.

Emily's mom—now *she's* old, with her hair in rollers half the day. And when it's out of rollers and she has *her face on*, Emily's mom looks worse. All her makeup sticks into the wrinkle-lines on her face. Powder-creases there. Her false eyelashes come unstuck and, half the time, are pasted onto her eyelids in precisely the wrong place. Like spider legs, Missy thinks, although she'd never say that to Emily. Emily thinks her mother looks fine and she spends most of her time rolling her eyes at Missy's mom when she hangs out at Missy's house.

"God, your mom's so weird," Emily says.

Susan's mother is pretty, in a bland way, but she's always at school, and so doesn't seem to have time to wash her hair or iron clothes or speak to anyone. She rushes through the house, holding books and smoking, pushing her glasses up on her nose. Everything in Susan's house is a disaster, sort of like Missy's house. Emily's house, however, is pristine. Missy's mother has said, "You could eat off the garage floor over there."

"Did you hear me?"

"What?" Missy looks at the floor. You couldn't eat off this one. She balances her knapsack on one shoulder. It is full of everything she will need for the sleepover in the trailer. An extra blanket in case it gets cold. A jar of cold cream because they have decided to give each other facials. Some nail polish for the manicures and pedicures (stolen from Shoppers Drug Mart last Wednesday). And two *Archie* comics and a *Teen Beat* magazine. Emily is supplying the candy and pop and chips. Susan said she'd bring sleeping bags and she promised not to bring the one her little brother threw up in last year when her family went camping. Besides all that, Missy has a change of clothes, her nightgown, and some underwear. She has also packed an extra athletic bra, even though she doesn't need more than one. She isn't sure if she'll fall asleep with her bra on, and in the morning they are supposedly going shopping at the mall so she'll want to have something clean. Although Emily and Susan don't wear bras yet so it might be awkward for Missy to take hers off in their presence. Or so she thinks. Missy isn't really sure. This is the first sleepover she's gone to since she's had breasts. Of course she has a toothbrush and hairbrush as well. And some other things that were in the bottom of the knapsack, things that she decided not to take out: a pink rock, a fake diamond ring, some hard candy, and lint. There's always lint. How it gets there is a mystery.

"I said I want you back by three o'clock tomorrow."

"Okay."

"Three. No later." Missy's mother turns back to the TV. "We're having Sunday dinner with your grandparents."

Missy starts to leave the house. She turns and heads towards the door.

"Hey, wait a minute." Missy's mother gets up from the couch. She walks unsteadily towards Missy and then takes Missy's face in her hands. She kisses her on both cheeks.

"Be good."

"I will, Mom."

"I love you."

"I love you too." Missy turns again to leave.

"And whatever you do, Missy," her mom says behind her, "don't sneak out of that trailer."

At Shoppers Drug Mart Missy is stealing nail polish. It is the Wednesday before the sleepover. Her mother is in the next aisle, buying tampons. Missy doesn't want to be anywhere near her. She puts a blue polish in her pocket and then looks around. She puts a pink one in the other pocket. No one is watching.

Missy's mother got caught shoplifting when she was fourteen. Missy is twelve. She thinks it's in her blood. Unavoidable. At least that's her excuse.

Missy's mother comes around the corner brandishing her tampons in one hand and two *Archie* comics in the other.

"You want these, hon?"

"Sure, Mom."

Missy can feel the weight of her pockets all the way up to the checkout. They are heavy and loaded down, as if she's carrying refrigerators in them. It's as if she's walking stooped. This is bad, Missy thinks.

But no one says anything. Standing in front of the store, Missy wipes the sweat from her forehead while her mother stops to light up a cigarette. At home Missy puts the blue and pink nail polishes in her dresser drawer under the old undershirts she used to wear before she got athletic bras. On Saturday she decides to take only the pink nail polish to Emily's as Susan will think blue is too weird.

It was Emily who shouted *Hey you* to the guy in front of Lee's All-Night Variety Store. He was walking in the dark on the other side of the road, walking slowly past them, they couldn't see his face. Just a beard, and a toque pulled down low. He was ageless. Hands in his pockets. He was sauntering. Even then Missy remembers his

I Still Don't Even Know You

hard shoes clip-clopped. Even then she remembers that he wasn't wearing running shoes like a normal guy. His shoes clopped slowly. He didn't look as if he could move fast at all.

"Hey you."

That's all it took.

Susan was carrying the licorice in a brown paper bag. She had one dangling from her mouth.

Emily had Freezies. She had three of them. Again, in a paper bag. Missy had nothing. Her mom didn't give her any money before she left. She was going to steal something but the Chinese guy behind the counter in Lee's All-Night Variety Store kept looking at her like he knew what she was thinking. She assumed he did. She assumed he was Lee.

It was midnight. Or around there. Certainly late. And dark. And the roads were deserted. Except for that guy walking slowly in the other direction.

Where was he going?

Where had he come from?

"Hey you."

"Shhh," Susan giggled. The licorice, red, dangled from her mouth like an obscene thin tongue. A snake's flicker. She gobbled it up, passed one to Missy. But just as Missy went to grab the offered candy, the man turned towards them, crossed the street in one huge clip-clopping run, and came straight for them, his hands out of his pockets now, his toque down over his eyebrows.

He was scary.

That's all that Missy could think. Scary and fast. And why was he wearing a toque in the summer? And a coat? And he ran with his legs stiff and his arms pumping. He wanted to get somewhere fast.

They scattered. All three girls scattered instead of sticking together. How many times had they been told to stay together and yet they took off in completely opposite directions, Missy towards Emily's parents' house, Emily up through the old apartment parking lot, and Susan down the hill in the direction of the school.

Missy picked the worst way to run. To get to Emily's house she had to sprint up the hill as fast as she could, then turn right, down the street, and then through the creepy path by the reservoir. Always dark. Always full of corners. You never knew who would be hiding there. God, all the times Missy and Susan and Emily had run through there screaming their heads off, afraid and thrilled. Even knowing the path was there, Missy kept going, because through all of the running and panting and yelling—she could hear Susan and Emily shouting far back there—Missy could hear the clip-clop of his feet behind her.

What did he want with her?

She hadn't screamed *hey you.* She didn't have any Freezies or licorice. She had nothing but the wind in her hair and her deep breath and her aching chest.

Run, run, run.

When Missy's mother says *don't sneak out*, it leaves a bitter taste in Missy's mouth. All the way to Emily's house Missy can taste it. Because they had planned to sneak out. Of course. But how could her mother know that? It's not like any of them had talked about it outside of school. Missy wonders if her mother has hidden some sort of tape-recording device on her. Maybe she hired spies in the schoolyard. Duncan or Phil? Those two are always trying to hang around with Missy and Emily and Susan, always sneaking over and scaring them when they are huddled together talking by the benches. But school has been out for two weeks. Surely her mother can't really know? She said it because mothers say those things.

Missy feels sick. Along with the bitter taste, there's the feeling of butterflies in her stomach. An itchy, awkward feeling. And her hands are shaking a little bit. Not too much, but enough for it to be taken as a sign.

Is it a sign?

Don't sneak out.

What the heck did her mother think? Of course they were going to sneak out. They were going to set up in the trailer in the carport, Emily's mother was even going to bring out a small TV for them to watch, she was going to have an extension cord running from the plug at the side of the house to inside the trailer. They were going to have flashlights and sleeping bags and pop and chips and candy and TV and nail polish and cold cream for the facials, and they were going to sneak out. If Emily was lucky, she was going to grab a bag of Oreo cookies as well. And they were going to sneak out. Around midnight. Late, at least. When it was really dark and when all the lights were off in Emily's house. When Emily's mother was in bed with her hair in rollers and Emily's father had passed out in the den.

That's what they were going to do. Of course.

Where were they going to go?

Missy doesn't know, doesn't want to know, doesn't want to care. She just wants to sneak out of the trailer with her two best friends, into the night, and have an adventure. But she knows they will probably end up at Lee's Variety. They always go there on the way home from school and Missy knows it's open all night (or why would it be called All-Night?). And Emily says she's going to get some money from her dad before he passes out. And Susan says she's saved up her allowance. They'll get candy and stuff and they'll walk around in the cool night and just look at things, look at lit-up windows, if anyone is still awake, and talk and tell stories about what's going on inside the houses. That's what they'll do.

They won't get in trouble.

They aren't bad girls.

Besides the shoplifting. But Missy figures that if you think about all the horrible things she could get up to in life, the shoplifting is nothing big. It's only a few nail polishes and occasionally a candy bar. The most expensive thing she's ever taken is costume jewellery and that was only a nine-dollar pair of cubic zirconia earrings.

Nine dollars. One hour of her mother's work day at Walmart.

During the pedicure Missy is feeling strange. Emily has her face smeared with cold cream and her hair up in a towel turban. She wanted to get cucumbers from the house and put them on her eyes but Susan wanted to get a pedicure too and so all three girls needed to be there to do each other's toes.

"Besides," Emily says, "there's no way I'm going outside with a turban on and all this guck on my face."

Missy laughs.

"Imagine," Susan says, "if Phil saw you like that."

Phil? Why Phil? Missy feels like she's missing something. Does Emily like Phil? Gross.

"God," Emily says. "That would be crazy."

"Let's call him," Susan says. "Let's call him and tell him to come over."

"No." Emily puts her hands on her face in shock and then realizes that she has smeared all her cold cream. She wipes her hands on her bare legs. The girls are all wearing shorts. It's hot and stuffy in the trailer and Emily's mom could get only one window open. She wouldn't let them keep the door open. Mosquitoes, she said, but Missy knows it's more about safety. With the door shut the trailer feels very safe. Like a sauna. Like jail.

Missy sighs.

"What?" Susan says. "Don't you like Phil?"

"No, of course not." Missy can't imagine liking Phil. He pushes her a lot, pokes her, steps on her toes. Occasionally he says *you're stupid*, or pulls her hair. Who would like Phil?

"We don't have a phone in here," Emily sighs. "And my mom would know if I brought it outside."

The girls continue painting each other's toes. Missy's stomach is roiling. It could be the pizza they had for dinner, or the nacho chips, or the three cans of pop, or the Oreo cookies, or even the ice cream cake Emily's mom had for them—like it was someone's birthday and not just a sleepover. Emily rolled her eyes and said, *Mother*, but Missy liked the cake and thought it was extra-special nice of Emily's mom to think of them. Although now she's feeling kind of sick.

Emily's mom came out to the trailer with this cake and her face was all shiny like she'd been crying, her eyes swollen, and she presented the cake on a tray and said, "Here you go," in this musical, magical, too-high voice. Emily said, "Mother." And then Emily's mom left and the girls had to eat all the cake really fast because it was melting so quickly. Then the tray sat in the corner and started to smell.

Missy gets up with her cotton-ball-separated toes, walks on her heels over to the tray, picks it up and opens the door and tosses it out onto the front lawn.

"That thing was stinking," she says.

Emily laughs. "Stupid cake. It's not my birthday."

"I guess it's our beginning-of-summer party, though." Susan looks dreamily up to the ceiling of the trailer. Missy can see the sweat in her hair, along her temples. She wipes her own face. "I wonder who will be in our class next year. I wonder if we'll still be together."

"Let's go out now," Missy says. "It's too hot in here."

"Our toes," Emily whines.

"When they dry," Susan says.

It is not quite midnight and the girls lie on their sleeping bags on the trailer floor and wait for their toes to dry in the hot, stuffy air. They are all a little tired. Missy can feel her bones sinking into the sleeping bag. There is a slight vomit smell coming from somewhere and she really hopes Susan brought the right sleeping bags.

But because it was Missy who said, "Let's go out now," it really is Missy's fault. All of it. Everything that has happened that night is Missy's own fault.

Serves you right, her mother would say. *For being so stupid.*

And then she would go on about how stupid she was when she was young and just look at what happened to her.

This is different, Missy thinks. This is the kind of trouble you couldn't predict getting into. The kind of trouble that just happened. Who knew he would run after her?

The man has passed by the car where Missy is crouching. He is on the street. She is in the driveway. The path to the reservoir and the road back to Emily and Susan lie in the other direction.

Missy thinks, How many people, kids, sneak out all the time and nothing ever happens?

The man is whistling now. Low and strange. A song she's never heard. Something old-fashioned. The kind of song her grandfather would know.

Her grandfather. He whistles in the work shed, fooling with his tools, and her grandmother is always in the house cursing her mother. Not good for anything. Dress like a whore. Drink too much. Smoke too much. Missy's mother doesn't do anything right.

No wonder she got pregnant.

Here is Missy, behind the fender of the car. The big dog in the window of the house behind her is going crazy, barking up a storm.

The man stops whistling and the dog suddenly stops barking and Missy can hear her breath coming out, shallow and ragged.

Go away, go away, go away, go away. It's all she can think.

One *hey you.* That was all it took.

"Come out, come out, wherever you are."

The clip-clop of his hard shoes. His toque. His beard. His hands in his pockets.

Susan and Emily are probably in the trailer now. They probably took the right path through the reservoir and not the wrong one. Missy didn't know there was a wrong path. She thought there was only one path. But it's so dark, so close to midnight, and she is so scared.

"Well, hello there," he says. Right there, beside where she's crouching. He is standing directly over her, looking down, a smile on his crooked face. She can see his teeth glint through his beard. She can smell him and he smells like a wet animal, like something wild and sweating.

Missy screams. The dog begins barking again. A loud, low bark. Missy falls back on her bum, her skinned knees in the air.

"Hush," the man says, and his face is contorted. "Hush."

He bends down to her and she stops screaming. Just like that her voice disappears. Her mouth is open but nothing is coming out. Missy can't hear the dog anymore either, as if the man has put a spell on the both of them.

"You're a good little girl, aren't you?" he says, reaching down to help her up.

Oh God, Missy thinks. I'm good?

This is how they sneak out.

First they tiptoe out of the trailer. They shut the door quietly behind them. Emily is nervously giggling and Susan is all bossy and scared. Missy is feeling good. It's cool outside and the air is fresh and she suddenly doesn't feel so sick. She looks at the cake tray on the lawn and smiles. It's a fine night.

Emily shushes and tiptoes and whispers and signals for them to follow her and they run quickly up the street towards the path to the reservoir. All three girls stand in front of the dark path. Trees on one side, backyards stretching out down the hill, a high wooden fence on the other side. The path is narrow. Too narrow for more than one girl at a time.

"You go first," Susan says. She is shaking.

"No, you."

"I'll hold your hand," Missy says.

"But if you hold my hand I can't run." Emily looks around. She looks back at her house and at the trailer. She has left the TV on in the trailer so if her mother looks out the window she will think the girls are still in there, watching. The trailer is a flickering, blue light.

"Okay, run." Emily bolts through the path, the other girls close behind, screeching quietly. Screaming in whispers. At the end of the path they start laughing.

"Oh my God, oh my God," Susan gasps.

Missy's heart is beating wildly. She swears she felt a hand reach out and grab her in the path. She says this and all three girls squeal with delight. And then they hold hands and skip to Lee's All-Night Variety Store at the bottom of the hill.

"This is so much fun," Missy says.

"A night to remember," Susan says. "That's for sure."

"My sleepovers are always fun," Emily says, and when the other girls look at her she says, "well, they are."

Once, when they got home from her grandparents' house, and Missy's mom sat down and proceeded to get really drunk, with her free hand she also reached over beside her to Missy on the couch, and she took her daughter's hand in hers, and said, "You know, Miss. You're the best thing that ever happened to me." She squeezed.

And Missy knew it was true.

There is a quick flash of white and brown and the man reels back and falls on the driveway. Now his feet are in the air instead of Missy's and the bottoms of his hard clip-clopping shoes shine with no tread. The barking dog from the house is not barking anymore because now the dog is that flash of white and brown that is pinning the man down and biting him. Another man stands in the doorway of the house in his dressing gown and shouts,

"Bingo, get down, Bingo!" And then he says, "What's going on? What are you doing in my driveway?"

But Missy is too far gone to hear the second part of that, and the growls from the dog carry her skinned knees, her bare legs, her pumping arms, towards the path for the reservoir, and she comes tearing into the dark path so fast that when she collides with Emily and Susan, who are running down the path to find her, they all start screaming like mad and crying and clutching each other, and Missy pulls them back through the path to the other side, shouting, "How do we get home? How do we get home?" and Emily and Susan turn back and race ahead, showing her the way, shouting, "The other path, the other path," as if Missy knew it existed before and was just dumb, until they are all collapsed in the hot trailer in the carport of Emily's house, the door shut tight behind them and locked, and there is silence once more except for the beating of their hearts, the gasping of their breaths.

Three girls lying still on their sleeping bags on the floor of the trailer, looking up at the ceiling at the flicker of blue from the TV.

It's three o'clock on Sunday and Missy is home and her mother is trying on clothes, worrying over everything she puts on.

"Oh God, she'll hate this, I know she'll hate this," Missy's mom says, rooting through the closet.

"It's okay, Mom," Missy says. "You look great. You always look great." She's tired. She didn't sleep at all. Missy notices her mother's fingernails are blue, the same blue colour Missy stole from Shoppers Drug Mart last Wednesday. Missy stiffens. She wants to go in her room and open her undershirt drawer but she's too afraid of what she'll find.

"I look fat," her mother says. "Nothing works right. Nothing is good."

"No. You look amazing."

On their way out, at the door of the house, Missy's mother looks back wistfully to the living room, to the TV, to the ashtray and empty wine glass on the table. Missy takes her mom's blue-nailed hand in her own pink-nailed one and squeezes hard. Her mother looks at her.

"God, you're getting tall. I barely have to look down anymore." She laughs. "Did you have fun last night in the trailer?" She laughs again. "Trailer trash. Oh, my mother would love that one."

"Yeah," Missy says. "It was good."

"Let's not tell Grandma you slept in a trailer, okay?"

"But it's a fancy trailer, mom. Real nice."

"Doesn't matter what kind of a trailer it is. Even if it's a movie-star trailer. Your grandmother... well...." Missy's mom stops and looks at her daughter. Right in Missy's face. Missy can smell cigarettes and toothpaste. "You're not like me, though," she says to Missy. "You know. You're nothing like me, Missy, and don't you forget it." She turns away from her daughter and straightens up, lifts her chest a little, puts on her game face. "You, Missy," she says with a sigh, "you're a good little girl. Aren't you?"

"Henderson Has Scored for Canada"

She's got her small hand balled tight in his large fist and they are walking towards Maple Leaf Gardens like it was any plain evening other than September 4, 1972. Her whole body is quivering, tight. Her mouth is moving in circles, saying things to herself that no one can hear. Saying, "Jesus, Jesus, Jesus," and "USSR," drawing the esses out like snakes hissing. Maggie doesn't know what USSR means, but she understands they are the enemy and she is about to see them skate out onto the ice like a pack of wolves. Daddy's holding her hand tight in his and they are joining the crowd now, walking in a flow like a river to the Gardens.

Maggie says, "Why's it called 'Gardens'? I don't see any gardens."

And Daddy hushes her with a quick tug on her hand. Maggie knows he's still angry at the loss in Montreal and angry at Mommy. He's talking again of Tretiak, of how that goalie, with his flimsy skates and weathered uniform, still managed to kill Team Canada on the first night.

"It was all about saving goals, not scoring them. Canada was stonewalled. They were out of shape and arrogant," Daddy says.

"Mommy wouldn't like it here," Maggie says. "It's too squishy."

"Huh?"

Tight up against the other ticket holders, the crowds surging, Maggie looks down at her shoes and wishes she had worn something more comfortable, something good for running. Because if these USSRs are as mean as Daddy says, she's going to want to start running, bolting it out of the Gardens and into the city streets, through downtown Toronto. She imagines them with fangs. She imagines them skating together, feet going back and forth like that street band she saw when they drove to the city for last year's Santa Claus parade, the skaters marching like devils, their blades slicing high above the ice.

Last night in bed Maggie had a dream about the USSRs. Last night she could hear Mommy moving about the kitchen and Daddy's silence like a scream, the house smelling like dirt and warm air. There was the sound of the wind in the dead cornstalks, again like snakes, saying USSR, USSR, and the chickens in the barn scratching wildly in the mud.

"Jesus," Maggie whispers when a large man bumps the top of her head with his elbow.

"Shush," says Daddy. "Where'd you learn to swear? Your mommy teaching you bad habits?"

They drove all afternoon to get here. They drove past their own measly cornfields, past their neighbours' farms, left Mommy at the house, alone—"You be alone when we come back, Janine. I'm warning you."— drove until Maggie fell asleep sitting up in the front of the truck, bumping and swaying, her nose full of the scent of hay and clover and chickens. She woke to the sounds of the city, an air brake squealing, she woke to find her daddy munching a doughnut, sprinkled, holding one out to her, the truck stopped at a rest station. He was waiting for her to wake up so she could pee in the stinky washroom. Waiting for her to wash the sleep out of her eyes, to get that sour, late-afternoon-nap look off her face.

"Good to sleep, Grumpy," Daddy said. "It'll be a late game."

Even though it cost a bundle, Daddy brought her here because Mommy said it'd do her good. Said it'd do him good to get both of them away from the farm for awhile. Away from the stupid corn which didn't grow this year on the long stalks. But Maggie somehow knew she meant get away from her. From that something that has to do with Mr. Reynolds from the bank. From Mrs. Reynolds coming by late one evening and talking in low whispers to Daddy and then Mommy walking out onto the porch and the yelling, starting. Mrs. Reynolds screaming *house-wrecker* and Daddy slamming doors. "What kind of a man are you?" she screamed. "Can't keep hold of your woman."

Mommy told Maggie the Summit Series was an important step for Canada, claimed patriotism would make things better somehow, that their faces in the stands would mean something to the rest of the world.

"Don't let them win," Mommy said. "It's bad enough. Things around here are bad enough without losing to Russia, too."

Holding Daddy's hand, Maggie doesn't want to be here. She doesn't want to mean something to the world. She wants to be home with Mommy, away from these people, away from the evil that's going to happen in the arena. Stepping into the building behind the burly men, she fears the pack of USSR men she assumes are waiting below the stands, silver blades shining like knives, slashing. She fears Mommy alone at the farm, the house creaking around her.

"The Bay of Pigs," Mommy said, "the Cuban Missile Crisis. And now Vietnam."

"What's that have to do with hockey?" Daddy said, and Maggie laughed because she imagined a great body of water filled with floating pigs. "What does any of this have to do with hockey?" And then Maggie imagined the Hudson Bay Company in town filled with pigs because the Hudson Bay Company was the only Bay she knew and suddenly she wanted a chocolate malted from the third floor by the children's department. She wanted to ride the pink elephant, bucking noisily in the corner by the washrooms. "What happens to the corn won't be changed by us going to Toronto." Mommy lifted her hands up and dropped them. "Things have to get better, Frank."

There is a sudden silence in the room.

"Seven to three, Frank," Mommy whispered. "All of Montreal in the stands."

Maggie looked at the clock. It was 6:30, not seven minutes to three. She raised her hand to point out the inconsistency. But they looked past her, through her.

"They'll win in Toronto. The Russians lucked out in Montreal. That's all it was. Blind luck."

"They'll win if you are there," Mommy said.

Daddy said, "Then they should have won with 18,000 in the stands in Montreal, Janine. Isn't that right? Two more people aren't going to make a difference. Besides, we don't have the money."

"Go, Frank."

"I'm a small person too," Maggie said. "Almost half a person."

"I didn't think you liked hockey, Janine."

"I hate hockey," Mommy whispered and Maggie echoed, "Me too," just so she could be like Mommy, just so she could say something that made some sense. Because she is a girl and Mommy is a girl and life moves like that, in circles. It's easy if it all makes sense.

And Daddy said, "Hockey isn't the worst thing in the world, Janine. There are things much worse."

"Not in front of the child. Jesus, keep her out of it."

"I don't want to leave you alone."

They are seated in Maple Leaf Gardens, Maggie shaking a little from cold, from excitement, the air a live cloak of anticipation around them, circling them. Maggie wanting so badly to know where the gardens are—the pretty gardens. Maggie was promised gardens and saw maple trees and tulips and chrysanthemums. Instead it is cold and bare and white in here. There are no flowers. Not even pictures of flowers on the walls. The attackers, Tretiak, Yakushev, Petrov, somewhere in the bowels of the arena, under their seats, waiting to come out and attack. Russia. USSR. Esses. Hissing wind in the cornfields. The smell of cigarettes and cold ice and sweat moving around her, Daddy's white knuckles cupped together.

"Not one crummy flower," Maggie says. "Stupid Gardens."

Mommy said last night at dinner, "Don't bring Maggie into this, Frank. This is our problem. Not hers."

"I'm taking her to Toronto is all," Daddy said, shovelling potato salad on his plate. "We'll go and see the game and then we'll come home. You told us to go, didn't you?"

"You will, won't you? You'll come home? I want you to come home."

"We will. Together. You'll be alone. You'll be alone here at the farm and I'll damn well bring Maggie home."

Mommy was somehow satisfied at this. Maggie cringing under the steel in her Daddy's voice, sucking the melted butter off her cob of corn, licking the salt and strings. The corn given to them by Mr. Malton on the next farm over. His corn grew big and sweet and healthy. Daddy won't eat the corn. Daddy looks at the corn on his plate and his mouth moves into a tight ball, his chin hard.

Daddy squeezes Maggie's hand tightly as they sit on the hard plastic seats in the arena. As they wait for the game to begin. Maggie doesn't know what is to come. The Zamboni cleans the ice. A Dominion advertisement on the side of the large machine spells out MAINLY BECAUSE OF THE MEAT. Daddy reads it to her because she asks him to. He'll do anything for Maggie. She is four years old, five after Christmas, and the hockey game stretches before her like the rest of her life. Mommy shops at Dominion. She buys meat there. And potatoes and carrots and toilet paper.

Mr. Reynolds, his huge bulk filling up the patio screen door, hugging up close to it and peering in at Mommy as she washes carrots in the sink, Maggie playing by the kitchen table, moving Barbie onto the farmer's wagon, taking Ken off because he's been riding long enough. Mr. Reynolds' eyes looking right through her mommy, peering through her clothing and her skin and bones, and her face blushing red, the freckles standing up.

"How are you doing, Janine?" His voice sending shivers around the house.

The corn didn't do well this year. A bug. A blight. A caterpillar. They won't tell Maggie what it is. They haven't time to fill her in on details. Something happened. Things aren't the way they should be. Mr. Reynolds runs the bank and her daddy owes him a lifetime of money. Mommy invites the man in for a tea and Maggie is told to go out to the barn, she is told to check on the chickens. Mr. Reynolds gives her a lollipop and a pat on the head.

Maggie, in the barn, thinks of Mr. Reynolds' daughter, Marilee, and how she always has a lollipop sticking out of her fat mouth. Marilee with those red bows in her hair and her face puffed up from eating. Marilee at the grocery store saying, "My daddy says you've got no money for clothes. My daddy says you're going under." And Maggie imaging her daddy swimming through fields of mud. Going under.

Daddy's up on his feet now, shouting something. The crowd is suddenly noisy. There was singing "O Canada," and then this. Maggie startles and looks down at the men on the ice. Too many men, skating furiously back and forth, chasing a puck. A puck so tiny Maggie can barely see it. And the sounds echoing. The chop of sticks, the swish of blades, the rush of wind. Maggie's breath is sucked out of her. Daddy says something about the two sets of brothers playing, how they'll work together because they are blood—Mahovlich and Esposito.

"Keep your eyes on Tretiak," Daddy says. "Keep your eyes on Phil Esposito."

Maggie is looking for blood on the ice but, again, she can't even see the puck. The men look the same in their clothes, their large bulks hunched over the sticks. They all have sideburns and long hair. Only some of them are wearing helmets. The game started so quickly and her mind was elsewhere and now she's lost the puck amongst the players' legs. The USSRs are not a pack of wolves but a wall, moving as one down the ice.

Sound surrounds her. Heads move back and forth. People arching, throwing arms in the air. Maggie didn't know the game would be so physical. It's like the playground on a hot summer day, kids moving furiously, the air pushed heavy onto their heads as their eyes, ears and mouths catch the movement of play.

First period over. Maggie breathes out and in.

Everyone worked together. Even the crowd.

Maggie thinks it was magic.

Daddy takes her to the hallway and lights a cigarette.

"What's a house-wrecker, Daddy?" Maggie asks.

The smoke creeps from his mouth slowly, Maggie watches it curl.

Export A written on the signs hanging around the arena. Maggie recognizes it from the pack in Daddy's front pocket. She knew McDonald's when she was fifteen months old, her Mommy told her. Back then she would say *fresh fries* whenever she saw the golden arches. Maggie is convinced she's reading now but her Mommy says she's memorizing. The Zamboni moves gracefully in the arena. Moving only Because of the Meat, Maggie thinks.

"It's none of your business," Daddy says. "It's not a word you should know."

"But it's two words."

"You're smarter than you think," Daddy says. He ruffles Maggie's hair and she likes his warm hand on her head.

Daddy doesn't have to ask if she likes the game. Maggie's eyes shine.

In the second period Esposito scores. Daddy was right. A brother. The 16,000 fans all rise together. A great wave. Maggie thinks it's like the corn blowing down in the wind, the stalks stretched forward, bending. The air swirling around them. Whoosh.

"Commies," some people shout. "Reds."

"Jesus," Daddy says. He shakes his head. He is going to say something long, Maggie can tell, but instead he says, "Come."

Daddy doesn't want to leave her alone in the stands and so Maggie follows him to the washroom and watches as he unzips in front of the trough and pees into the flow of water. He pees with the other men, more than a dozen men, they all watch their urine flow towards a hole in the trough, mixing together. Like pigs standing and feeding on her grandpa's farm in Barrie. Is this the blood Daddy was talking about? Blood brothers. Like animals. Is this the Bay of Pigs Mommy mentioned? Maggie wishes she could join them but there is something distinct about being a girl, something hidden and solitary. Her mommy sits on the toilet and Maggie can only hear the rush of water leaving her body. She can't see the yellow line it makes in the bowl. There are things hidden that Maggie wonders about.

Third period. Canada scores. Then USSR. Then Canada and Canada again. The brothers working together, using their teammates. Tretiak alone on the other side. Mahovlich falling somehow on top of the USSR goalie and slipping the puck into the net. Maggie sees it all, finally. Surrounded by it, the game becomes clear to her. Her daddy shouting, on his feet, his face red-pleased and hot. Maggie's breath comes back, steady and simple. Her heart swells, her hands clench. The excitement around her is like the dip in the hill on the road near their house. A quick rise and then sinking, stomach hitting her back, her bones mashed into the vinyl seat where Maggie rides looking out the window at the blue sky and white clouds.

And then everyone is leaving the Gardens in a mass. Horns on the street outside. Black night. Maggie is sleepy. Daddy picks her up and she leans her head on his shoulder. The men around her clapping each other's backs, shouting *we did it*. Maggie hears a tin voice, a loudspeaker, from inside the arena—*restoring confidence in the Canadian people*. Her daddy's tight grasp around her body as he walks, a lightness in his step. A whistle in his mouth as they drive the long road back towards the farm. Talking about the game. Play-by-plays. Explaining to Maggie what she thinks she already knows. Maggie is too excited to sleep. But then, hours later, Maggie awakes to a guttural choke coming out of Daddy's throat as they drive past Mr. Reynolds' truck, its headlights glowing, passing them on the highway, coming back from the direction of their farm.

The darkness settles into the kitchen where Mommy, her head in her hands, is crying.

"My God, Janine," Daddy hisses.

"There's things you don't know," Mommy says. "You just don't understand."

"They won, Mommy," Maggie says, sleepily. "You should be happy." The dead corn in the field bends down in the wind. The chickens scratch the barn floor. Maggie hears this amplified. The silence is loud.

"We won?" Mommy says.

Daddy slams the kitchen door and disappears out into the wind and the blackness.

And then there is Winnipeg. Maggie watches on TV, curled into a ball on the living-room couch. Tie. Tie score. Daddy wears a tie when he goes into Toronto to apply for a loan.

Vancouver knocks Maggie down. Makes her sad. She's become addicted. She likes hockey more than sugar now, giving up dessert so she can sit and watch the game. So she can watch the flow of people as their heads move back and forth to watch the skaters move. It's her mommy's way of making her healthy, making her pick one or the other. But Maggie would rather be part of this something that will pull them together, that will pull people together. Something this big and strong, a force like a tornado. Sugar means nothing anymore. Her mommy puts a fire in the fireplace to save on heating the house. The Russians win and Maggie skulks around the house for days, angry at everyone and everything, smacking the barn cats as they rub against her legs. Phil Esposito almost swore at the fans and Maggie feels like swearing all the time now. She feels like saying the words she hears her daddy saying when he's out in the field.

Daddy's tie didn't work. He says that the man at the bank just laughed at him as he closed the file folder on his big desk.

There are hot days and cold days. There are days when Maggie runs through the withered corn laughing and chasing her friends who come to play. There are days she huddles under the covers on her bed, afraid to go outside of her room, afraid to hear nothing, a spark about to burn, a bomb about to explode, that silence that fills the house, top to bottom.

The corn is full of holes. It is small. Not fit to feed the chickens, even. Daddy walks through the stunted fields each day with a look of pure hatred on his face. Maggie watches as he plucks off the rotten corn and throws it to the ground. He looks like he wants to take his cigarette and burn down the land. Daddy is in the barn with the damn chickens, and Maggie feels that he might put his foot through one of them, kick it high in the air like the football he sometimes throws with their neighbour on hot summer days. She sees something in his eyes, knows the anger in his voice. Mommy's at the bank again, asking Mr. Reynolds for more money. She's asking him not to take the house, the fields, the chickens. She's wearing nylons, her hair in a bun, lipstick patted carefully with Kleenex.

The long break after Vancouver, it seems like forever, where the days and nights flow into one, where she hides in the barn in the increasingly cold afternoons and lies in bed at night listening to her mommy trying to talk to her daddy. Listening to Mommy's low rumbling sound. She wanders the fields, keeping behind her daddy, a piece of grass stuck between her teeth, listening for the ins and outs of his breath.

The Goon Squad, The Canadian Mafia, the headlines screamed. Skating in Stockholm to get used to the ice, to get their anger and frustration out, chase it away like demons under the bed. Then just as suddenly, Moscow, Moscow, Moscow.

Moscow over the TV set. Maggie sees the strange domes, the spires in the air. Luzhniki Arena. *Luzhniki*. Maggie tries hard to pronounce the word but the word always twists her tongue, curls it, until she can't help but spit. Phil Esposito slips on the ice and then gets up and bows, like a ballerina, a graceful dip. The crowd roars. Jockey, Turtle Wax, Motorcraft, Heineken Beer. Daddy reads the side-boards and tests Maggie's memory.

"Of course they won," Daddy says after the game. "They're on their home turf."

"What's turf?"

Daddy turns off the TV and settles back into the rocking chair, his hands up behind his head. He rocks quickly.

"Turf is where you live. Turf is what you have here," he points to his chest. "Inside of you."

"Don't be silly, Frank," Mommy says. "Turf is grass, Maggie. Like on a golf course. All the same length."

"There's no grass in Moscow," Maggie says. "I know that. Just big open squares and lots of grey buildings."

"It's a black-and-white TV set, Maggie," Daddy tells her. "Of course everything is going to be grey." And quietly. "Turf can mean many things too complicated for you to understand."

Maggie sees a cow covered in green moss. A moss-cow. She goes to bed at midnight, wakes early, replays hockey in her mind. Wishes she had seen the first game in Montreal. Wishes she had known then what she knows now. The Russians aren't wolves anymore, they aren't a wall, they are coyotes, sneaky and unafraid.

It seems to Maggie that everyone is watching hockey. In town the storekeepers have their TVs on the counters. They watch the replays, the commentaries, the breaking news. They talk about Bobby Hull when he wasn't allowed to play in Winnipeg, or Serge Savard when he is hobbled by a hairline fracture. Over and over again Phil Esposito assures Canadians that the players are giving 150%, and Mrs. Mercer at the Becker's Store feels good about that. Tretiak, Tretiak, Tretiak. His name uttered with a spit, said in disgust, distaste, but also said with envy and admiration. Players who are enemies every season in the NHL are working together now.

Mommy touches Daddy's head as she passes him in the living room and his eyes water. His cigarette flares red, an angry eye, always glowing. He spends several days helping out on Mr. Malton's farm, cleaning up after the corn harvest, coming home sore and tired, callused and mad. He still won't touch the corn, won't eat it when it's placed on his plate, but Maggie goes through each sweet, buttered cob, back and forth, like she's typing a message to God on her grandpa's typewriter.

Maggie says, "Moscow," to the librarian one day and they both raise their eyes to the ceiling and watch the fan circle amidst the spiderwebbed rafters. The librarian crosses her fingers and Maggie crosses hers. There's a holy feeling in the air. Like an electrical storm coming softly and slowly towards them. Like the rumbling of a train. The librarian stamps Maggie's books and lets her out of the library to wait for Mommy on the street.

Two more miraculous wins for Canada and, even though the corn didn't grow, Maggie smiles brightly wherever she goes.

And now it is the final game and Daddy said he would come in after he feeds the chickens to watch with Maggie.

"Don't ask him for anything, Janine," Daddy said to Mommy when she left in the truck for the bank again. "Don't go. I'm telling you. I want you to stay here with your family."

"I have to go, Frank."

"No. Don't go." Daddy pounded on the truck. "Stop this." He almost cried but Maggie chose not to see this. Maggie's mommy chose not to see this too. They both turned a little as Daddy made a stabbing punch-motion at his face to wipe the wet.

Maggie said, "Ask him for a lollipop. He always gives me a lollipop."

Mommy held the steering wheel tightly and turned quickly out of the driveway, away from the farm. Daddy walked out to the barn, his shoulders raised high and tight, his neck stiff. He sniffled like he was coming down with a cold.

"Daddy. It's on," Maggie shouts from the back screen door. "Foster Hewitt is on. He's talking."

"Of course he's talking," Daddy's voice comes clear from the barn. "I'll be there in a minute."

It seems to Maggie sometimes that her mommy and daddy are the only ones around whose lives haven't been completely overtaken by hockey. It sometimes seems as if they would much rather be doing other things. They would much rather be in the fields or sitting at the kitchen table with coffee, saying nothing, looking everywhere but at each other's faces. Maggie's mommy would rather be cleaning the house and changing the sheets on the beds, cooking biscuits and scraping together leftovers into pots to make what has come to be known as garbage soup.

Maggie sits cross-legged on the carpet in front of the TV. Since game five Maggie has fallen in love with Paul Henderson. Number 19. It's a childish love. There is no sensation that she is a girl, he is a boy. It has nothing to do with that. It's not the kind of love she feels for Joey Tanner, that tough boy in the playground. It's more like the love she feels for the Friendly Giant and his soothing recorder. An all-consuming, careful kind of love. In game five Henderson knocked himself out on the boards and still he struggled up and continued to play, continued to score. He was determined, like last summer when the chicken pecked the barn cat's eyes and still the cat came at the chicken, mouth open, eyes tearing and bleeding slightly, hissing wildly. Maggie has a love for Paul Henderson that somehow means he will save her, take care of her. He will make sure she is taken care of.

"Can't kick a man when he's down," Daddy said when Henderson lay motionless on the ice. Daddy was sitting on a kitchen stool looking into the living room, following the game out of the corner of his eyes. Mommy said nothing then. She hummed a tune. Washed dishes in the sink. Her long hair hiding her flushed cheeks.

Daddy comes in from the barn now carrying his hunting rifle. He props it up against the counter. He has grease on his hands. Maggie watches him scrub it off in the kitchen sink, using dish detergent. He leans back against the stove and wipes the sweat from his eyes. His shoulders are still tight. His smile is strange and crooked. Maggie shivers.

"It's on. You're missing the game."

"I'm coming."

Maggie watches her daddy as he crosses in front of the TV and settles on the couch. He lights a cigarette and draws deeply on it. Maggie suddenly misses the Export A advertisements in the Gardens. She wishes she were there, in the arena, with the men and the smells and the sweat and the peeing trough. She wishes she could be there to feel that heavy excitement in the air. The kind of feeling she gets on a swing when she is pushed high into the sky, so high her bum leaves the seat and the chains clink noisily in her hands. She wants to feel the way the crowd moved together, how everyone worked together to make the game happen, to make Canada win.

Penalty after penalty.

"Let's go home," the Canadians in the stands chant when the

filthy Russians put the cheating referee from game six into the game. Switching officials. Daddy says it's rotten.

"Cheating," Daddy says.

"Not fair," Maggie says, although she doesn't quite understand why. "That's not fair."

"It never is," Daddy says. "Life isn't fair."

A dog barks somewhere outside. From Mr. Malton's farm where they've taken the day off work to watch the midday game. Daddy was invited there but didn't want to go.

"I might be heading out soon," Daddy says. "Would you be okay by yourself for a bit?"

"No," Maggie says. "This is the last game. You can't leave me alone."

"Just for a bit. Not long."

"Mommy never leaves me alone. You can't leave me alone. It's not fair."

"Mommy's Mommy."

"What?"

Maggie imagines Mommy sitting in front of Mr. Reynolds' desk at the bank. She imagines Mommy sucking on a lollipop and smiling nicely.

"I'll only be gone for a little bit. You'll be fine by yourself."

Parisé, given a penalty, suddenly lifts his stick to strike down the referee. But then he pulls up from the swinging motion just in time. Maggie sucks in her breath. She is conscious of her daddy's heavy breathing. He is slumped on the couch. His cigarette, ash building at the end, hanging off his fingers, unsucked.

"Look at this," Daddy says. "We're going to lose."

Daddy rises from the couch. He goes into the kitchen and takes the rifle from its space beside the counter.

"Don't go," Maggie says. "Jesus."

"I don't want to lose," Daddy says. "Don't swear."

"We won't lose. If you stay here and watch we won't lose, Daddy."

"Not even for a minute. I've never been a good loser."

"Don't leave me," Maggie says. "Who am I going to watch the game with? I'm not old enough to be left alone. You're not supposed to leave me alone."

"Just for a minute. It won't be long. I'll come back soon and then we'll go somewhere. Maybe we'll go on a vacation or something. Anywhere you want."

But as he walks towards the side door Maggie can hear Mommy pull into the driveway in the truck. She hears the door slam and Mommy walk, shoes crunching, up the gravel path to the house. Daddy stands alone in the kitchen, one hand on the side door, the other hand holding the rifle. His face is sweaty. He looks like Maggie feels when she has to pick between a Popsicle or ice cream. When she wants both, but has to decide.

"Mommy's home. You can go now. She'll take care of me."

Maggie knows the kids at school are watching the game. She knows this because Susan Jessup told her last week at the park in town. She said that the school was setting up a TV in the gym and the kids were all going to sit nicely, backs straight, and watch hockey. They were going to sit with straight backs or their principal, Mrs. Pearson, would poke them hard on the shoulder, one by one, and tell them to stand in the hall. Susan said they weren't allowed to talk, they could only watch the game and cross their fingers and pray that Canada would win. Maggie wishes she were there with them, in the large gym she's seen only once—Thanksgiving last year, lines painted on the floor, basketball hoops in the air above their heads, Mommy dropping canned beets into the box by the gym door, beets for poor people who like beets—she wishes she could hold Susan's hand and pray quietly when Yakushev ties the game in the second period. Next year Maggie will be in school but by then it will be too late. The game will be over. It will all be over.

Mommy comes, breathless, into the kitchen. She spots Daddy standing still and she rushes over to him, rushes slowly, like running through water at the pool, and she takes the rifle out of his hand.

She places it carefully on the kitchen counter and then she wraps her arms around him, wraps his arms around her, rubs his back and touches his hair. She whispers in his ear, soft sounds. Like she's calling in the chickens. A cooing.

Maggie watches the Russians score at the end of the second period. She feels sick to her stomach. She hasn't eaten lunch, no one has thought to feed her, and her stomach is rumbling wildly, sloshing around empty.

"This will help, Frank," Mommy is saying. "This will get us by for awhile. Maybe a month or two. We can get jobs then. Get jobs through the winter and then move on. Maybe move away. We could move into Toronto and work there. We can start again. Straighten this whole mess out. I can type, Frank. I can type fast. Your father has that old typewriter in the back room. I can practise until I can type twice as fast as I can now."

She is holding a slip of paper in her outstretched hand. She has moved away from Daddy now and is standing between him and the rifle, holding out this paper as if she's offering him a poisonous snake. Maggie sees the tremble in her mommy's hand. The paper wiggles.

"I want a peanut butter sandwich," Maggie says. "And a root beer."

"I'll make that," Mommy says. "Frank, move. Say something."

Daddy stares hard at the door. His eyes move towards the paper Mommy is holding out. He stares back at the door.

"I'm hungry," Maggie says. "No one feeds me anymore."

"I'm back, Frank. Everything is okay."

"Did you get me a lollipop? Where's my lollipop?"

"He just gave me the money, Frank. No strings attached. It's over. He won't take the farm yet. Not yet. We have some time now, some time to—"

"Did he give you a lollipop?" Maggie asks. "He always gives me a lollipop and tells me to go out to the barn. He touches my head. I don't like that. I don't like for people to touch my head. Except Daddy."

"He just gave you the money, Janine?" Daddy's voice is low. A rumble.

"Yes. It's over."

"Quiet," Maggie shouts. "The game is on again. Daddy, come quick."

"He just gave you the money? That's it? Just like that? He didn't want anything for it? Is that what you're telling me? He handed over money and you did nothing, you didn't take off your clothes, you didn't fuc—"

"Shut up." Mommy looks down at her stomach. The paper still hanging on the end of her outstretched fingers. She uses her other hand to flatten the dress she is wearing to her breasts. She breathes deeply. "Yes, Frank. He just gave me the money."

Daddy watches the motion she makes. The way she touches her breasts briefly.

Maggie watches the motion. "Why would Mr. Reynolds want you to take off your clothes?"

Mommy's hand touches the material slowly, touches the mounds of her breasts. Maggie doesn't understand this but somehow Mommy's hands moving over her woman's breasts is a movement that sums everything up, puts the world neatly into a paper package and sends it flying through space.

"Shhhh." Maggie puts her finger up to her mouth and turns back to the game. Canada scores. "They scored! You aren't watching. You both aren't paying attention."

Maggie hears the slap. She doesn't see it. She hears what she later realizes is her daddy's hand moving in a long arch, fast, fully controlled, towards her mommy's face. The sound is like a water balloon hitting the pavement. The sound is like a clap of thunder or like the sound the watermelon made at the farm picnic last year when Mr. Malton's kids threw it off the barn roof. Maggie turns towards her parents and sees her daddy standing in the same position. Her mommy is holding her hand up to her face, a red welt rising, tears coming softly out of her eyes. The paper is lying on the floor between them.

Canada scores again. The light doesn't go on over the net. Maggie turns back to the TV. Suddenly, Alan Eagleson bolts out of the stands and tries to get to the ice. The Russian police surround him. The Russian fans whistle instead of boo.

"Look, look," Maggie shouts. Team Canada skate together to free Eagleson. They take him to the Team Canada bench. Maggie starts to cry.

"I don't know why he did that," Maggie says, crying. "I don't know anything. I wish you'd both sit down and tell me what's going on."

"Oh, honey," Mommy says. She walks towards Maggie with her arms outstretched.

And Daddy walks out of the house, the kitchen door slamming shut. Maggie can hear him walking out towards the fields. She knows that he walks past the barn, through the grass, into the useless corn. Maggie lets her mommy hold her and she cries. She doesn't know why she is crying. She looks up into her mommy's face and sees the slap mark of her daddy's hand. She looks back into the kitchen and sees her daddy is long gone.

And then Mommy looks up and into the kitchen.

"Oh my God. Frank?"

She releases Maggie, stumbles towards the door.

"No, Frank. No. Jesus."

"Mommy?"

But the shot is loud. It echoes through the fields. Maggie's mother running quickly, falling, frantic, bumping her hip against the kitchen stool, screaming, out of the house.

"No. No."

"Here's a shot," Foster Hewitt calls. "Henderson makes a wild stab for it and falls."

Mommy running through the horrible corn. Maggie standing

now, looking at the TV. Paul Henderson. Looking at the kitchen towards the window over the sink, watching Mommy running. Maggie moves towards the kitchen and then back towards the TV. Towards the kitchen. Back. TV. Kitchen.

Suddenly, Mrs. Reynolds' car pulls up in front of the house. The car door slams shut. Crunch of gravel. Maggie watches as the woman, a sun hat on, her face red and swollen like her daughter's, starts to walk up to the front door. Maggie sees Mommy running. Maggie can see everything. The back window, the front window, the front door, the TV, Paul Henderson skating so hard he looks like he might fly. Maggie looks around, confused, and feels shivers move through her body and the house. A cool breeze, like just before a storm when you know the air is changing and the rain will come crashing down. Mrs. Reynolds pounds heavily on the front door.

"Janine," Mrs. Reynolds shouts. "I know you're in there."

"What was that noise?" Maggie whispers.

USSRs.

Russians.

Hiss.

"Jesus," Maggie says. "Hockey."

Foster Hewitt, breathless now, "Here's another shot. Right in front."

Daddy's rifle is missing from the kitchen counter.

"The Summit Series," Maggie whispers to herself. Esses. "Paul Henderson." Words that feel like candy on her tongue.

Maggie doesn't know which way to turn.

TV.

Window.

Mrs. Reynolds at the door.

Paul Henderson.

Daddy.

The rifle is gone.

Mrs. Reynolds knocking hard. Mommy running, chasing something. Both Mommy and Mrs. Reynolds screaming something.

"Janine. Open up."

"Frank, no."

Foster Hewitt shouts, "They score! Henderson has scored for Canada!"

"Oh," Maggie breathes. "Bang. We won."

And the silence around her is suddenly a roar.

Credits

Versions of the following stories were first published in these publications: "Five Old Crows" appeared in *Little Black Dress*, Polygon Press, Scotland, 2006. "Mary-Lou's Getting Married" appeared in *The Capilano Review* (1999) and in *Best Canadian Stories: 2000* (2000). "I Still Don't Even Know You" appeared in *Taddle Creek* (2006). "Drowning" appeared in *Descant* (2000). "Be Kind to Your Children" appeared in *Taddle Creek* (2001). "Making Spirits Bright" appeared in *The Globe and Mail* (2001). "Christmas Has Gone to the Dogs" appeared in *The Globe and Mail* (2000). "The Cat" appeared in *Quarry Magazine* (1998). "Martin" appeared in *Border Crossings* (2001). "Hunting for Something" appeared in *Canadian Fiction Magazine* (1999). "Henderson Has Scored for Canada" appeared in *Story of a Nation*, Doubleday Canada,(2001).

Acknowledgements

With extreme gratitude, and in no particular order, to the following:
Stu, Abby and Zoe, Charlie Foran, Margaret and Edward Berry, David and Nicola Berry, David and Beverly Baird, Wayne Tefs for his keen eye, Jamis Paulson, Sharon Caseburg and all Turnstone staff for their kindnesses, Karen Kretchman and Charlotte Convery, my Trent University, Humber College, and Ryerson students, Conan Tobias at *Taddle Creek* magazine, Douglas Glover at *Best Canadian Stories*, Simon Beck from *The Globe and Mail*, Susie Maguire, Rudyard Griffiths and The Dominion Institute, all Canadian literary magazines in general, my agent Hilary McMahon at Westwood Creative Artists, Dawn and Dave Carr, the women writers who lunch in Peterborough (you know who you are), Jonathan Bennett and Wendy Morgan, Natalee Caple, and finally the animals, Buddy, Sebas and Max.